VALLEY U

REBECCA JENSHAK

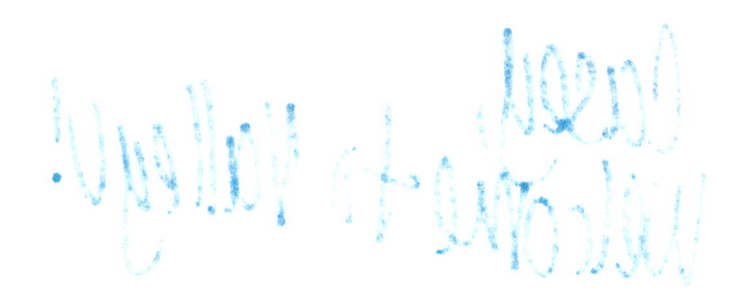

© 2022 by Rebecca Jenshak
All rights reserved. Except as permitted under the U.S. Copyright Act of 1976, no part of this book may be reproduced, distributed, transmitted in any form or by any means, or stored in a database or retrieval system, without written permission from the author.

Rebecca Jenshak
www.rebeccajenshak.com
Cover Design by Lori Jackson Designs

The characters and events in this book are fictitious. Names, characters, places, and plots are a product of the author's imagination. Any similarity to real persons, living or dead, is coincidental and not intended by the author.

Created with Vellum

THE ASSIST

SMART JOCKS BOOK ONE

You know those stories where the smart girl tutors the dumb jock? This isn't it.

Blair:
What's the probability of insulting the one guy on campus I need to help me pass statistics?
If I knew, I wouldn't be standing in front of Wes Reynolds begging him to tutor me.
Basketball player, sexy, arrogant, always sleeping through class... these are the things I knew about him.
What I didn't know is that he is a seriously smart jock.

Wes:
What's the best way to get rid of the peppy and unrelenting girl that keeps asking me to tutor her?
If I knew, I wouldn't be staring at her tan legs and attempting to teach her statistics.
Sorority girl, fine as f**k, determined, ball buster... these are the things I knew about her.
What I didn't know is that she is all the things I didn't realize I wanted or needed.
Or that one semester with her would change everything.

PROLOGUE
BLAIR

Three Years Ago

"Who run the world?" Gabby and I scream the lyrics at the top of our lungs. Top down on her cherry-red convertible, music blaring, hair blowing across our faces, we pull out of the high school parking lot with the first day of classes behind us.

"One more year, Blair. One more freaking year, and we're out of this place," she says when Beyoncé stops singing.

"You don't think you'll miss it? Even a little bit?"

She shoots me a look that questions my sanity. "No. We're going to Valley U, we're going to study hard, party our asses off, and then, when we graduate, we're going to start some fabulous female only business and end up on the cover of *Forbes* or *Vanity Fair*. You and I are meant for more than Suck Hill."

Her enthusiasm is contagious. I want all those things, truly, but it's Gabby who is counting down the days until we can leave our small town of Succulent Hill, which Gabs lovingly renamed Suck Hill. I've always liked the community and friendliness of living in our hometown. Not Gabby. She's been dreaming of moving to Valley and attending the university there since we were in middle school.

Bringing the car to a halt at the four-way stop just outside of our neighborhood, she turns the radio down. There aren't any other cars as far as the eye can see, but we continue to idle in place. I meet her serious gaze. "What's wrong? Are we out of gas again or something?"

"Promise me we're getting out of this town."

I laugh off her words. "I promise."

She grabs my wrist and pulls on the friendship bracelet I made in eighth grade. The ratty thing made of purple thread from my mother's sewing kit still hangs on my arm. A matching one dons her wrist. It's become a symbol of our relationship and the promises we've made. "I mean it, Blair. You and I are getting out of this place. We're going to make something of ourselves. Run companies, have someone fetch us coffee, live in fabulous downtown apartments, and have brunch dates after Pilates on the weekends."

"I know. We've only been talking about it forever."

I don't understand the sudden urgency of her words. We should be enjoying our last year and planning what we'll wear to prom or what we'll put in the senior time capsule. College is a year away and there's so much to do before then.

"Swear it. Swear you're going to do it with me."

Gabby's perfectly styled blonde hair blows in the breeze like a commercial for Vidal Sassoon. It's easy for people to laugh off her ambitions as the rambling of a pretty girl whose been handed everything her entire life. She *is* beautiful, and she *has* been handed her share of privilege, but only I know how strong her desire to rule the world is. I don't believe in my own dreams nearly as much as I believe in hers.

I nudge her with my elbow. "I swear, Gabs."

My faith in myself is shaky, but I believe in Gabby, and with her by my side, I know we're capable of anything.

Dark clouds off in the distance warn of a monsoon storm rolling in just as Gabby parks in front of her house and closes the convertible top. "Sure you don't want to come with me tonight? Rachel's back to school pool party is going to be epic."

"Can't. We're going out to dinner to celebrate my dad's birthday."

Outside of the car, I breathe in the smell of rain in the distance. The wind has already picked up, and I'm looking forward to the heavy gusts and downpour that won't be far behind. When Gabby and I were little we'd talk on the phone through storms, anxiously waiting for the puddles that would be left behind so we could splash and play before the dry desert ground soaked up all the water. I shuffle toward my house, just three houses down from Gabby's. We've been neighbors our whole life, best friends too.

"You could sneak out after." Her sea-blue eyes light up with mischief.

"No thanks. I'm not risking getting grounded two weeks before the pep rally."

She kisses the air. "Fine, loser. I'll text you later."

"Later, Gabs."

I send her a wave over my shoulder and make my way home. Thirty minutes later, I'm sitting at my desk, watching the rain trickle down the window of my second story bedroom, when I see Gabby's car pull away from the curb. With a sigh, I pull out my history textbook and turn to the assigned reading.

If my best friend could see me now, she'd roll her eyes and call me an overachiever. I'm probably the only person sitting at home tonight instead of attending Rachel's party. Tomorrow everyone is going to be talking about it, and all I'll have to contribute to the conversation is the formation of the Provincial Congresses during the American Revolution.

I struggle to focus on the words as my brain tortures me with daydreams of how much fun everyone is having. Still, an hour passes and I'm almost done with the first chapter when my mom knocks on my door.

"Blair, honey."

I stand and stretch. "Come in."

I grab my purse, prepared to celebrate my dad's birthday. My brother and his new wife are meeting us. It should be fun. Although, it doesn't really compare to a pool party with all the coolest kids at SH High.

When I open the door, mother's face is not of happiness or celebration. My stomach drops, and my body tenses in preparation of receiving bad news.

"Mom, what's wrong?"

"Honey, it's Gabby."

———

People talk around me. My brain catches and fixates on single words. Hydroplaned. Unconscious. Critical. Brain Trauma.

I don't care about any of it. I just want to see her. I want to march back there and see Gabby pop up out of bed and tell me it was all a big joke to get me out of the house for the night.

But it's two long days and nights of sleeping in the waiting room before they let me into her room in the intensive care unit. I've been warned about the trauma of the accident, internal and external, but when I see her lying in bed bruised and covered in bandages, I run to her side and grab her hand. It's only relief and happiness that brings the tears to my eyes as she tries to smile around the cuts on her face.

"Gabs."

She opens her mouth and then closes it, frowning. "I..."

"What is it?"

A single tear slides down her face. "I can't remember your name." More tears fall, and each one breaks my heart a little more. "I know you're important. I can feel it in here." She slowly lifts a casted arm to her chest and taps. "But I can't remember who you are."

A nurse in blue scrubs enters the room. "Gabriella, I need to take you downstairs for a scan."

The use of Gabby's full name opens the floodgates, and every emotion I've felt in the past forty-eight hours assaults me at once.

"I'll come back, Gabs." I squeeze her fingers lightly and then flee like a coward out of the room.

Tears blurring my vision, I stumble into the small sanctuary of the hospital and let the sobs wrack my body. I curse God and then apologize and send up a quick prayer. I'm not sure where I stand on God, but this doesn't feel like the right time to snub divine intercession.

A small head pops up in the front row, and I halt two rows back, leaving a respectable distance between us. A girl, no more than ten, turns and offers me a small smile. I wipe my face and nose and give her a half-hearted wave before settling into the pew. The wood creaks beneath me, and I gaze forward to the huge cross nailed to a cement block wall.

Little feet skip down the side of the room and a mass of blonde ringlets bounces beside me. "Hi, I'm Sunny."

Of course she is. She exudes light and cheer, which is saying something in this shitty excuse for a house of worship.

"Hi, Sunny. I'm Blair."

"I like your bracelets." Her eyes track my arm as she studies the colorful adornments with wide-eyed wonder.

"Thank you. They're friendship bracelets." My voice breaks and I swipe at new tears.

"It's okay to cry," she says with reassurance. "Momma says we gotta cry out all the sadness to make room for hope to grow. Positive thinking attracts miracles."

The door to the chapel opens and a woman looks in, finds Sunny and motions for her. "That's my mom. Gotta go." Sunny doesn't wait for my goodbye, she runs into the arms of her mom. I watch as the frail woman hangs her head low and clings to the bundle of sunshine.

It's too much, so I turn forward, giving them privacy and letting Sunny's words take root. Positive thinking attracts miracles, huh? I close my eyes and say another prayer because, devoted believer or not, I'm willing to call in favors just in case, and then I push away all negative outcomes and only allow myself to imagine the future with Gabby by my side.

1

BLAIR

Present Day

"Well, that pretty much seals my fate." Vanessa flashes her test, showing off the red F at the top of the paper. "Wanna come with me to get a drop slip?"

"No. Don't leave me alone in here, V. It's only the first test. We can do this." My attempt at a pep talk fails miserably. Probably because I'm simultaneously suppressing a groan at my own hostile red letter. Circled and underlined for emphasis. As if I needed more than the large D staring up at me as an indication I hadn't done well on our first statistics test.

We wait for our classmates to filter out of the large auditorium, and judging by the grim expressions and mutterings about the evil professor, we aren't the only ones who did poorly. A small comfort, I suppose.

So much for my perfect GPA, and so much for winning over Professor O'Sean. He's the program coordinator for the accelerated MBA track that I'm applying to next year. It's just a hunch, but I don't think failing his class will help me get in. College hasn't been exactly what I envisioned when Gabby and I planned our futures all those years ago. Actually, that's too bland a statement. It hasn't been all bad, but so far, this semester royally sucks. I feel guilty for even thinking those words. It'll all work out. I just need to buckle down and study harder. Think positive.

Vanessa nudges me while we trudge up the stairs. She leans in to whisper, "My last chance to ogle the man candy."

I follow her slight head nod to the back row, which is occupied by three members of the university's basketball team. I'd like to think I would have noticed the trio, built like the nationally ranked athletes they are, even if Vanessa hadn't pointed them out each and every class. But the last month has been a haze of homework and studying. I'm not sure I would have noticed them even if they'd sat beside me. If it doesn't involve classes, caffeine, or sleep, I don't have time for it.

Their skin tone varies from light to dark, as does their hair color, but each one is tall and muscular. Decked out in athletic gear, they look like they walked off the set of a Nike commercial.

The one on the end closest to the aisle has his foot propped up on the seat in front of him, a black walking boot covering it completely from just below the knee on the right leg. His arms are crossed over his chest, and the blue Valley basketball shirt he's wearing is bunched up around his muscular arms and pecs. A baseball cap is pulled low so it's covering his eyes, but it doesn't matter—it's obvious whatever lurks below is as good as the rest.

"Why is the line moving so slow?" I step to the right to see what the holdup is. I have places to be, and it's lunchtime. What's the hold up?

"Slow down and appreciate the view with the rest of us," Vanessa retorts.

I glance ahead and behind, seeing nothing but necks careening and eyes darting to the back row. The line out of the class moves at rubberneck speed. Has this been going on since classes started three weeks ago? How had I not noticed the ovary explosion they caused? I'd assumed it was just Vanessa being well, Vanessa. Apparently, no one was immune to their beefy muscles and chiseled jaw lines. Except me.

I would be proud of that fact if my grade backed up the time I'd spent not noticing hot guys. I've actually been paying attention to the professor. I need this class. Correction. I need an A in this class. Now, I wish I'd used my time more wisely like V.

"Everyone is staring at them."

"Duh, look at them. They're the best part of this class," Vanessa says loud enough that the girl behind us snickers.

She's right about that. Each one of them is stop-and-stare worthy, but my eyes are pulled back to the guy on the end. The top half of his face is a mystery – covered by a white university hat. But his lips are fantastic and full in a way that no lip injections could replicate.

I'm still starting at him when his teammate, the one sitting closest to him, reaches over and flips up the baseball hat, revealing a pair of heavy lids. He rights his hat and then reaches for the paper on his desk. My eyes follow his long fingers and bulge at the big red letter A that is underlined and circled just like mine. The underline and circle treatment of my D seems a lot less hostile now, so that's something.

But what the hell? This guy is sleeping during class and still gets an A?

"Why does he even bother coming to class if he's going to sleep through it? There's no way he earned that grade without help. How are the rest of us supposed to compete with the private tutors and special treatment that's afforded the student athletes?" The words spill from my mouth before I can censor and spin them in a more positive way.

We push out of Stanley Hall and join the rest of the students bustling between classes at Valley University.

"Bitter much? What happened to your peppy optimism and we-can-do-it attitude?"

I wear my positivity like armor. Smile on and words of wisdom on deck, I'm always the first person to look at the bright side to hide the insecurities and fears I don't dare speak.

"It just had a heavy dose of reality. Even the jocks did better than we did," I say as I stare down at my yellow chucks.

When I look up, she gives me a sympathetic half-smile and shrugs. "I don't know about the basketball team, but Mario says the baseball guys get ridden pretty hard about grades."

"I'm sure they get ridden hard, all right."

Vanessa's eyebrows disappear under her long bangs. "That is the weirdest thing you've ever said. Never repeat it."

She's effectively lightened my mood, and I hip check her playfully. "Speaking of riding them hard. Where is Mario? He's usually waiting like a puppy out here."

On cue, Mario comes into view. He's jogging to get to V as quickly as possible, as if it's been days since he's seen her instead of fifty minutes.

"We're going to lunch at University Hall after I stop by the registration office. Come with?"

Not even a full month into the semester and my roommate has already managed to snag a boyfriend. Mario may be a jock, but he seems different. He doesn't have any of the asshole, holier-than-thou narcissism I'd expected. He's pursuing V hard, walking her to and from every class, bringing her flowers, and taking her out on date nights, the works. I'd knock his adoration and classify him as a stage-five clinger if he weren't so handsome and sweet.

Wearing his practice clothes—a cutoff T-shirt and baseball pants—accentuates the whole all-American, tan, blond-hair, blue-eyed, good-guy thing he has going for him. Bonus points that Vanessa is completely smitten. I know this because she's trying way too hard to convince me otherwise. Case in point, inviting me to tag along on their lunch date.

"Can't save you from love today. I'm heading to the library to study."

"That sounds positively boring," she says over her shoulder as she skips off to meet him halfway. They come together, hugging and kissing, completely oblivious to the people shoving around them.

Gross.

Except it isn't. It's actually really sweet.

As skittish as I am about the opposite sex these days thanks to the last guy I trusted, Mario has given me no reason to doubt his intentions. And I refuse to let one asshole taint my view on every other guy for the rest of my life.

Speak of the devil.

My phone vibrates in my pocket, and I fight back the urge to press Ignore.

"Hello?" I answer cheerfully as if the man on the other end isn't the absolute worst.

"Where are you?" He wastes no such effort on niceties.

"I'm on my way," is the only thing I say before I hear the line disconnect.

With a heavy sigh, I head to the library. David paces the front entrance. His dark hair is tousled perfectly and emphasizes the crisp white dress shirt. He stands out among the other students who are dressed more casually. I used to like that about him, how he stood out amongst the crowd. Now, it's just another thing I despise.

"You have it?" he asks before the double doors have even closed behind me.

I bite back every mean and awful thing I've thought about the man in front of me. Polished and handsome on the outside. Horrible and ugly where it matters.

I hand over the folder, keeping my mouth closed.

He opens it, absolutely no regard for its contents. He can't fathom his actions having consequences, and he's made me all too aware of the ramifications of every single action I've made.

"Jesus, David, you could wait to inspect it until you get back to your room. It's all there. I wrote the answers on a blank piece of paper, so you can fill the worksheet in with your handwriting."

"We aren't in fucking high school, Blair. The librarians aren't sitting around looking for suspicious activity. As long as you keep your mouth shut, no one will ever know."

I grind my back teeth.

He snaps the folder shut and holds it in one hand at his side. "Professor Shoel assigned a five-page paper on a classical music composer. It's due next Monday, but I need it Friday so I can go over it and make sure it sounds like me. The last one you wrote sounded too girly."

Because a *girl* wrote it.

"How much longer are you going to do this to me? I'm failing my own classes, I can't keep up."

Desperation clings to my voice as if I could be anything but desperate.

He sneers, turning his handsome features cold and sinister until the outside matches the inside. "Would you rather I share your nude selfies with the world? Maybe that's what you wanted all along, for me to pass them around and give everyone a little taste."

My stomach twists with shame and regret. "Those pictures were for you, my boyfriend. You know I never meant for anyone else to see them."

"I'm sure you tell that to all the guys, but I'm not buying it." He leans in close, and I hold my breath as if not breathing in the scent of his expensive cologne and mint gum could take back everything. "When I feel like you've learned your lesson, then we're done. You got a problem with that, Blair?"

I hate that I'm in this position. Hate that he put me here. But, mostly, I hate that I don't have the balls to knee him and tell him to go to hell.

"No problem," I mumble.

2

WES

JOEL PULLS the Tesla into the garage and Z and I pry ourselves out of the tiny sports car. The rest of the team is already here and the splashing and music from out back filters through the house. It's a hundred and eight degrees in Arizona today. August was worse, but we're nearing the first day of fall, and I could literally fry an egg on the hood of the car. Shit isn't normal.

I miss the Midwest humidity. Never thought I'd utter those words.

Sometimes, I'd like to come home to a quiet house instead of the craziness of our non-stop party house, but I get why our place is the hang out.

The White House, which is what it was dubbed because it's white, it's huge, and it was purchased by the university president. Our house is only a few blocks from campus and right across the street from Ray Fieldhouse, making it ideal to walk just about anywhere we need to go—not that we had to thanks to my gimp foot and handicap parking. The only perk of being injured.

The White House is nicer digs than anyone else has. Fuck, this house is nicer than the one I grew up in. The only place I've seen that's nicer than this house is Joel's parents' estate. Estate as in it's too fucking big to just be called a house.

But the pool is really why they're all here. Well, that and the stocked fridge.

I swipe a cold water and head out to sit under the mister. Z grabs a protein drink and follows, taking a seat next to me off to the side and away from the pool hangers.

"Welcome home, roomies," Nathan calls from the pool. He has a cigarette dangling from his mouth and a beer in hand. It's barely noon. On a Monday.

I shake my head at him. I'm not pissed he's drinking and smoking. I'm pissed he's doing it in front of the young guys. He can handle himself. I'm not sure about the freshman.

I turn my attention to Z. "Getting in today?"

He grunts something in response. I've never seen Z get in the pool. We give him shit about it, but I honestly have no idea if he doesn't like getting into the water because it's usually filled with lots of people or because he can't swim. I can't imagine there's anything he can't do.

Quiet. Grunting. Out of the limelight. That pretty much sums up Z off the court. On the court, he's a whole different person. People who have never seen him play assume all kinds of dumb shit about him solely based on his mammoth size, or as he would put it, a big, beautiful black man. The fact that he walks around wearing his headphones oblivious to the world and rarely speaks more than a word or two at a time also doesn't help.

Once people see him play, though, it's like seeing someone in their natural habitat. He's smart, quick, and loud. Dude doesn't shut up on the court.

Shaw tosses one of the ball honeys—Charlene? Charla? Carla?—into the air, and her high-pitch squeal makes me want to cover my ears. There's a whole posse of girls standing in the shallow end, being careful to keep their hair and makeup water free. I wish I were a bigger asshole because I'd really like to go dunk the whole lot of them and watch the chaos that would ensue. Lucky for them, I only think this. Also, I'm not doing a lot of swimming these days with the boot and all, so I just sit back and admire the view. I'm annoyed, but I'm not blind.

So yeah, I'm a grumpy asshole. I haven't always been, but getting injured senior year—the year I was supposed to take the team all the way. Yeah, that would make even the nicest guy go a little douchebag.

The rest of the team mills around, swimming, lounging, drinking, eating all our damn food.

I drain the water bottle and drum the plastic container on my leg.

Bored.

Restless.

Joel appears at my side and flings himself down, cracking a beer open in the process.

"Rookie is out of control. I can't wait until you're back. Freshman needs to be put in his place."

My eyes go back to the freshman rookie who is front and center in the pool, tossing girls up and lavishing in the attention.

"Three more weeks. Fingers crossed."

"Good because we're screwed if we're depending on Shaw to get us the ball. I know it's supposed to be some big damn deal that he's playing two sports, but shit just makes me nervous. Twice the risk of injury and half the amount of focus."

I nod in agreement. "I'll talk to him and to Mario. I'm sure the baseball team has the same concerns."

"Wanna have a little fun with them?" Joel's attention is focused on the pool and pure mischief coats his expression.

"What did you have in mind?"

"Remember my freshman year when you guys made us crash parties and run plays?"

A chuckle rumbles in my chest. Being a freshman sucked in so many ways. My rookie year, the upper classmen mostly just made us do things like carry their gym bags and act as water boys. Fuck, I'd been so glad to be a sophomore and for a new crop of guys to take the heat. Joel and his class had been an obnoxious batch of freshmen and we'd increased the torture to knock down their huge egos. Come to think of it, Joel's class was a lot like this year's rookies.

"You thinking of taking them out tonight?"

"Yeah, but I think we should elevate – take it to the next level."

Shake my head. "We have practice in the morning, so don't elevate it too much. Coach'll kick our ass if we show up with a bunch of hungover rookies. Exhibition is coming up, and he's chewing Tums like candy."

"Live a little, Reynolds. It's your senior year. We're doing it up right."

"We're? You still got another year."

"Yeah, but it isn't gonna be the same without you and Z. This feels like the last year of something great. Something none of us will ever forget."

Shit. He's right. The season is shaping up to be the best year of our lives, and I'm itching to get out of this damn boot. It's making me cranky.

"Yo, Shaw." My voice booms across to the pool, and he lifts his head slowly, taking his damn time. A chin tilt is the only acknowledgment I get.

"Get me a beer."

Joel cackles. "My man, you don't even drink during the season."

"Rookie doesn't know that."

"No. No. No. Come on, guys. That's sloppy."

Sitting in a plastic chair on the sidelines with my booted foot propped on another, I bounce the ball back and forth under my knee. Back and forth, back and forth. I can't tell if it's making my nerves better or worse. I don't need to be here. It's torture, but there's nowhere else I'd rather be. This is my team. I may be injured, but they're still my responsibility.

"Fifty free throws and two miles on the treadmill and call it a day. We have a big week coming up. Talent only goes so far. Focus. Repetition. Heart.

Already having about a gazillion shots in for the day, I head to the weight room. I can't remember the last time I did leg day, and I've never wanted to squat and dead lift so much in my entire life. I pass Mario and a few of the baseball guys leaving as I enter.

Athletes have our own weight room, but we share it between all the different sports. It's huge—easily big enough for three or four groups to be in here at any one time, but we've all got our own styles. Football guys can't be in here without grunting and talking smack. The swimmers spend more time gossiping like old ladies than lifting. The basketball team likes the music turned up so loud there isn't much of an option to chat.

"Reynolds. Still gimping around, huh? When's the cast come off?"

Mario's guys keep going with a nod in my direction.

"Three weeks. Can't freaking wait."

"Thank the fuck. Those chicken legs of yours are getting damn near embarrassing."

I take his jabs in jest. Mario and I have been leaving our blood, sweat, and tears in this room for years, and we both know I have fucking great legs.

"Give me a few weeks, and I'll be squatting your pansy ass under the table."

"We'll see." He wipes his forehead with a towel and tosses it on his shoulder. "We're having a party at the house next Thursday. Be cool if you guys stopped by, haven't hung out in a while."

"Yeah, I'll let the guys know. Speaking of the guys, how's Shaw doing? Team's worried about him splitting his time. I am, too, if I'm honest. We're gonna need him to sub in some this year. Need him to be ready."

"I hear ya. I don't like it, either, but he's the best damn relief pitcher we've had in years. I'll keep an eye on him as best as I can while he's with us."

"Ditto."

Fucking freshman has two babysitters and almost fifty teammates between the two sports, and he's still shaping up to be the biggest pain in the ass I've seen in my four years.

3

BLAIR

Three days out of the week I work at the small campus café in University Hall. In addition to the café, University Hall houses the university bookstore, a mini convenient store, and a sub shop. Untying my blue apron, I lean on the counter completely exhausted after the lunch rush.

Coffee and a pastry totally counts as lunch in college making it our busiest hour. College kids - we're nothing if not lazy creatures of convenience.

"Hey, Katrina." I let out a sigh as my replacement arrives, signaling the end of my shift.

"Rough day?"

"The worst," I admit. She places a hand to her forehead and then swipes a strand of hair out of her eyes. Katrina is the same age as me but has a total mother-hen vibe. Maybe because she *is* a mother. She brought Christian in with her once. He is adorable, but he's also the best birth control ever. Katrina has her hands full between classes, working, and raising a little man by herself. Puts my own crap in perspective.

"It's nothing I just failed my first statistics test."

"Oh, that sucks. I'm sorry."

"Thanks."

She looks up to the ceiling. "What's the quote you're always writing about failure?"

"We learn from failure not success." I roll my eyes. "I know. I know. But I don't have any clue how I'm going to get an A when I'm already struggling a month into the class. The first month is supposed to be easy."

"You get what you work for not what you wish for." She recites another one of the quotes I often write on the to-go cups.

"It feels more like a suck it up, buttercup kind of day."

She pulls a cup from the counter and fills it with our house brew before handing it to me. "For the road."

I shake my head but grab a sharpie and write the quote on my to-go coffee.

"Another night of disappointed faces when they realize the quote girl isn't here."

That makes me smile. I love that I've been able to add a little bit of positivity. We've all got our struggles and I want to be someone that builds up other people.

The quotes were my idea. A random scribbling when I would notice someone looked like they were having a bad day or seemed stressed. Eventually they became something people looked forward to and I started writing them on every cup. It really isn't so hard to tell who needs tough love or an inspirational pick me up based on their demeanor or tone when they order. The quotes on the sides of the cups have become a part of the café, and it's a legacy I'm proud of.

I trek back to the sorority house with determination and resolve. I won't just ace statistics, I'll destroy it.

Suck it up, buttercup.

Two days later as I'm preparing for class, my inspired mood is appropriately deflated. Another late night of studying and homework leaves me pessimistic and petulant. I hate who I'm becoming. I've worked too hard and have come too far to crumble under pressure.

I decide to dose myself in positivity. Maybe if I feel good about how I look, some of those good vibes will soak into my attitude. I pull on my favorite yellow sundress and matching chucks. With a nod at my reflection, I'm off.

The large auditorium is made up of a semi-circle of three sections that face the podium, which stands front and center. Since Vanessa dropped the class and left me alone in my misery, I opt to sit in the back on the far right.

At exactly one minute before class begins, the eye candy arrives. Kudos for getting my head out of my ass to notice the trio of jocks. Vanessa would be proud. Honestly, what has my life become that I'm so overwhelmed with schoolwork that it took so long for me to appreciate hot guys without Vanessa to point them out?

When Professor O'Sean takes his position behind the lectern, I sit straighter in my seat and attempt to give him the kind of attention I usually reserve for the first week of class, jotting down nearly every word that exits his mouth and tallying the number of times he pushes his glasses up with his middle finger. Is he trying to flip us off or is it just a happy coincidence?

I'm able to focus on independent and dependent events for six minutes and fifteen seconds before I find my gaze wandering across the top of the lecture hall. My eyes go directly to the jocks. One in particular. Foot propped up on the seat in front of him, baseball hat pulled low. His teammates are next to him looking bored out of their skulls, but at least their eyes are open.

Honestly, how did this guy get an A? His tutors must be amazing.

When class is dismissed, I hurry out and then pace the sidewalk.

I can do this.

I *have* to do this.

I turn and face the massive fountain that sits in the center of the quad and take three deep breaths. When I turn back to Stanley Hall, it's just in time to see the three basketball players finally emerge. Statistics is the first class I've had with any of our college's nationally ranked team. They seem to stick together, though, always travelling in groups.

"Hi, excuse me." I smile brightly and step directly into their path.

They exchange a confused look but slow down instead of trampling over me like a bug, which they could very much do.

All five feet and three inches of me stands taller. I make eye contact with each of them, trying to look friendly and not at all intimidated, which I'm not . . . nope, not at all, and then lock my gaze with the sleeper's. He's the shortest of the three, but the intensity of his navy blue eyes makes it hard for me to find my voice.

"I'm Blair, we have statistics class together." I wave toward the building behind them in case they don't even know what class they just came from. Apparently, I am still bitter about the grade.

"Wes," he says as he shrugs his backpack up higher on one shoulder. "This is Joel and Z."

"Nice to meet you." I look to each of the guys and then back to Wes again, silently communicating he is the one I want to speak to. They don't get the memo. "Wes, can I talk to you for a minute?"

"We'll meet ya at the car," Joel pipes in, and he and Z leave me alone with Wes. It's only slightly easier to think without all three of them staring at me with rapt interest.

"What's up?"

"I was wondering if you could tell me who does tutoring for the team? I noticed your test grade the other day, not that I was trying to see it or anything. Sorry, that sounds horrible. I just happened to glance down as I was walking by your desk. Honest mistake. Honestly."

Deep breath, Blair.

"Anyway, I didn't do so well, and I really need an A in this class.

Does the team have someone specifically, or do you guys use the tutor center?"

His eyebrows pull together, and he shifts his weight to his left side, making me conscious that standing here talking to me is probably causing him pain.

Join the club. This whole interaction is excruciating.

"I'm lost. You want information on the tutor center?"

The hot Arizona sun shines bright and sweat trickles down my back. "Just information on the tutor or tutors you're using . . . for statistics."

"You think I have a tutor?"

"I'm sorry. I wasn't trying to be rude, but it's just you're sleeping through class."

He crosses his arms over his chest in a silent challenge. The neckline of his shirt pulls down, revealing a hint of tan chest underneath. Annoyed is a good look for him.

"You don't have a tutor?" The question is no more than a mumble. Or maybe I just can't hear it because my pulse is pounding in my ears. I open my mouth several times and then promptly close it when I can't find the words to apologize. He smirks as he watches me grapple with the realization that I've made a very wrong, very humiliating assumption.

Uncrossing his arms, he takes one step in the direction his friends went. "Tutor center is on the first floor of the library." He points in the direction of the campus library, making me feel about a foot tall. "I'm sure someone there can help."

As I watch him walk away, admiring his gait that's somehow sexy and confident even with the boot, I wonder—statistically speaking, of course—what are the odds that the guy sleeping at the back of the class could not only pull off an A but also manage to get that grade without help?

I have no idea, probably because I'm failing statistics. My guess, though? Not good.

———

I ARRIVE BACK to the scene of the crime, aka statistics class, with a cup of coffee, a new pen to inspire better note taking, and a determination to hide from Wes and company. I slip in five minutes early so I can grab a seat and be wholly enthralled when they show up. I don't fancy myself important enough that they'd seek me out, but my humiliation has big plans of cowering and hiding for the rest of the semester.

As if my body is now connected to my mortification, I feel the exact moment they enter the classroom.

Wes Reynolds, Joel Moreno, and Zeke Sweets are quite a trio. Yep, I looked them up. I'm calling it research, but in reality, I just wanted to have all the information on the guy I'd thoroughly insulted. They sit in the middle section at the very top, giving them a bird's eye view of the entire class. If Wes's eyes were ever open, would have been nearly impossible to be out of his line of sight. I'm not invisible, but it's as far away as I can get.

Zeke pulls his red headphones down and rests them around his neck as he squeezes his large frame into the seat. According to everyone I asked (more research, of course), Zeke is already rumored to be going pro after this season.

Wes wears a glare that would frighten small children . . . or grown ass women because I slink down in my seat as I continue to watch him. I have a hard time looking anywhere else, glare be damned. He's unbelievably gorgeous. Hell, they all are. Even Joel, who hasn't looked up from his phone, is strikingly handsome with his black hair and bronzed skin.

When Wes glances around the class and his blue stare lands on me, I become very interested in my notes from the last class, reading over them with a fervor I should have tried before the last test.

When we're dismissed, I hang back, waiting for the last row to leave before making my way up the stairs, but when the auditorium is nearly cleared out and the three musketeers haven't made any move to leave, I'm left with no other choice but to suck it up and hope they don't notice me.

Joel nudges him as I approach. Nothing gets past that guy. It's as if he's Wes's eyes and ears. As Wes's dark blue eyes land on me, I plaster on a big smile and decide to be the bigger person. "Hello."

Wes stands, awkwardly making his way to the aisle and holding on to the back of the chair for support. A flash of pain crosses his handsome features as he meets me on the stairs.

"Ball Buster Girl."

"I'm sorry about the other day. I just assumed . . ."

"That I was a dumb jock who couldn't possibly get a passing grade without the help of a tutor or tutorsss?" He emphasizes the plural version with a hiss as he trails me out of the auditorium. As we come to the door, he steps close and pushes the handle, swinging it open and holding it with one large hand. A gentleman. Interesting.

"To be fair you haven't made much of an effort to look like someone who is trying to get a good grade."

We stop on the sidewalk, and I'm aware of Joel and Zeke hanging back and giving us space. Wes adjusts his hat, lifting it so I get a glimpse of the dirty blonde hair matted down like he'd slept in the damn hat. Right, he had . . . just now.

"I could ace that class even if I never showed up."

"That's an awfully bold statement for the first month of class."

He shrugs. "Any luck finding a tutor?"

"Not yet, but I'm sure I'll have no problem finding someone who passed statistics with their eyes open."

His lips part, and his straight, white teeth peek out. "Good luck with that."

I shove my ear buds in and put on my favorite podcast and head toward the library. By the time I get to the tutor center located on the first floor of the campus library (already knew this without the help of Wes, thank you very much), I've turned my humiliation into focused anger.

Okay, so I jumped to conclusions too quickly, but if he can get an A with his eyes closed, surely, I can manage with a whole lot of determination and a tiny bit of help.

I'm still bristling at the way his indigo eyes laughed at me. He could have politely set me straight instead of acting as if I'd personally attacked his intelligence. Okay, maybe I had, but I mean, how was I supposed to know that the guy sleeping at the back of the class somehow magically aced the first test without help, which I'm still not entirely convinced he did.

A text from Gabby momentarily pulls me from my foul mood.

GABS: Still coming down next Wednesday?

ME: Of course I am! It's your twenty-first so we're going out!

SHE DOESN'T TEXT BACK, which tells me she isn't exactly on board with my plan to celebrate her twenty-first but knows me well enough to know I'm not going to take no for an answer.

I tuck my phone away as I walk to the tutor center's front desk.

"Hey, Blair, what are you doing here?" Molly, a sophomore sorority sister, asks from behind the sign in area.

"I have a question for you." I lean against the counter and pull out my ear buds.

"Shoot." Molly places both elbows onto the counter.

"What can you tell me about tutors for the athletic teams on campus?"

She scrunches her nose and tilts her head to the side. "Are you interested in being a tutor?"

"No, no. Nothing like that. I just wondered if you could tell me who tutors the athletes. Do they have their own private tutors, or do they come here for help?"

"I'm not aware of any tutoring services specific to the teams on campus. I suppose they could have personal tutors, but I've never heard of it. Why?"

"So, they come here?"

"We don't get a lot of athletes in here despite the assumption they need it. I mean, no more than any other group."

Great, I really am a profiling bitch.

Molly rattles on, "There's a few guys from the football team that come in regularly. Baseball team, softball team, wrestlers . . . yeah, I guess as far as I know the ones that need help come here."

"What about the men's basketball team? Do any of them come in for tutoring?"

She brings her thumb to her mouth and bites on the pad of it while she considers my question carefully. "Not that I can think of."

Damn.

"Do you guys have anyone for statistics?"

She grimaces. "Must be rough if you need help."

I nod. "D on the first test."

"Ouch," she says as she flips through papers hanging on a clipboard. "We have Sally and Tom in today, they both tutor math. I think they mostly do algebra and calculus, but I could put you in the schedule and you could meet with one of them and give it a try. Interested?"

"Sure. Why not? Got anything now? I'm done with classes for the day, and I don't want to come back to campus this afternoon if I can help it."

"Looks like Tom is free after his current session. You can hang over there." She nods to a section of chairs and couches pushed to one side of the room. "He should be done in ten minutes or so."

I stop short of the waiting area, spying the men's basketball schedule on the wall with a picture of the team decked out in their uniforms. The guys stand stoic and unsmiling, and my eyes drift first to Wes. He stands in the back row, wearing jersey twelve. His legs are hidden by the guy standing in front of him, which makes it impossible for me to see if he's wearing the boot. My research didn't pull up any information on his injury, so I don't know if it's recent, what he did, or even if he'll be out for the season. I'm suddenly very curious about Wes Reynolds.

In truth, I've paid very little attention to any of the jocks since arriving at Valley. Freshman year, I'd barely looked at anyone who wasn't in a fraternity. Greek life became a home away from home, and there was something exciting about finding a guy who had the same sort of passion for his fraternity brothers as I had for my sisters. And, of course, fraternity guys love nothing more than they love freshman pledges.

By the end of sophomore year, the guys at socials and parties started to blend together and Vanessa and I'd stopped choosing our weekend activities based on frat parties. We plan on moving out of the sorority into an off-campus apartment next year. I'll always treasure my years at the sorority, but I'm ready to have my own space.

David had been the quintessential frat guy, and I'd fallen for his charm and good looks before I'd realized what a monster he is beneath the shiny facade. Too little too late. It isn't as if I think all frat guys are douchebags based on one bad experience, but it's like getting food poisoning at a restaurant. Even if it was the cook's fault, your brain associates the restaurant itself with a horrible experience and you aren't likely to go back anytime soon.

When Tom finally waves me over, I'm so hopeful I could burst. But my optimism only lasts a few minutes. I'm not an idiot. Far from it. I get the basic principles of business statistics. I've read the book and memorized definitions. It's the real-world application that is just out of reach. Math word problems were the devil in sixth grade, and they haven't gotten any easier no matter how much I study.

Molly catches me on my way out. "Any luck?"

"No." I exhale a deep breath. "There has to be someone on campus who tutors statistics."

"Did anyone at the house have O'Sean last year?"

"I asked around. Nothing."

"I'll see if anyone here knows anything," she offers. "Someone has to have something on him. Old quizzes or tests. I've heard he's old-school and still does everything on paper."

Of course. Why hadn't it occurred to me sooner? Wes must have gotten his hands on tests from someone who'd taken statistics last year. O'Sean seems exactly like the type of professor to re-use the same material every year. That has to be the answer. Wes isn't sleeping through class and magically learning by osmosis. He already has the answers.

4

WES

"Rise and shine," Joel says as he nudges me. I'm not asleep. I wish I were. My eyes are closed, hat pulled down, but there's no sleep to be had.

"She's coming back for more." The tone in his voice is almost inspired.

I don't have to look up to know who he's talking about, but I do anyway. She's the most entertaining thing about this class. Open my eyes and lift the hat, turn it backward so my view isn't the least bit blocked.

Today she's wearing little pink shorts that show off tan legs, yellow tennis shoes that don't match but somehow work, and a bracelet with a little charm around her left ankle. It's too small to make out, but I stare anyway. Her brown hair is pulled up in a high ponytail, and she has a megawatt smile plastered on her face. A big bow on top of her head is all she'd need to look like head cheerleader of my high school fantasies.

"Wes, hey, can I talk to you for a second?"

"What's up?"

I'm hella impressed by the balls on this chick. She's put her foot in her mouth, not once, but twice, and damn near insulted the entire student athlete population, but she keeps coming back. She has determination and grit. I admire that about her.

I also am not in the least bit offended by her assumption that I'm a dumb jock. I'd be lying if I said I wasn't surprised she came right out and asked who my tutor was, but I know exactly what it looks like. I've fed into the stereotype for years, doing nothing to make it seem otherwise. Well, nothing but get straight A's.

"I have sort of a favor."

"What's up?" I stand to walk with her out of the class.

"The tutor center was a bust. I know you said . . ." She looks like she's choosing her words carefully. "Do you have old study notes or tests from previous semesters?"

"Still convinced I'm not capable of passing on my own, huh?"

"I'm sorry, really, no offense. I just want in on whatever study materials you're using. I can't afford to fail another test. What's your secret?"

The secret? I'm fucking smart. Photographic memory smart and statistics is my whole world, but I can't resist messing with her.

"You know, saying no offense doesn't make whatever you're saying less offensive. It just makes you feel better about saying something offensive."

Joel snickers behind me. I just can't resist fucking with her. She's making it too easy.

"Sorry. I'm really so sorry. What about the other guys on the team? Anyone have any awesome math tutors who aren't available to us non-jock students? I can pay."

"Couldn't say for sure, but I don't think so. Most the guys hold their own academically." I lean in catching a whiff of her hair. It smells good—like sugar cookies or candy canes or something sugary sweet that I want to sink my teeth into. "Shocking, I know."

Her shoulders slump in defeat, and I can tell she's finally accepted that I have no answers for her. At this point, I almost wish I knew of someone to send her to. I don't exactly travel in circles that clue me in on secret study sessions and underground tutor societies.

"Thanks anyway." She gives a little wave with the hand clutched around the strap of her backpack.

Joel catches up to me, and we watch as she crosses the campus toward the library. "Dude. That chick..."

"I know," I say, and we continue to stare after her completely awe stricken.

"Quit gawking after the poor girl and let's go. I'm hungry." Z's voice pulls at me just as Blair disappears from sight.

When I turn, Z's grinning like he heard the entire exchange, despite the fact he has his headphones on. Sometimes I wonder if he even has music playing or if he just uses them as a deterrent. I don't have the heart to break it to him that he's intimidating as fuck and probably doesn't need another reason for people not to engage.

Back at the house we sit around the television watching ESPN and devouring the chicken pasta shit that Joel's mom dropped off earlier. She has taken it upon herself to keep us fed and our pantry stocked. Several times a week we come home to find casseroles in our fridge, index cards with cooking instructions taped to the top of the tin foil.

"Why do girls insist on using eight emojis for every text?" Joel asks without looking up from his phone. His fingers tap at top speed on the damn thing.

"I dunno," Nathan says from the floor. He's alternating sets of push-ups and sit-ups. That's Nathan for you. One minute, he's cramming nicotine and alcohol in his system, and the next, he's doing bonus workouts. I guess it evens itself out. "It's up there with using text slang when it isn't any shorter. Using the number two in place of the word to saves what? Like a half second?"

"I deduct two IQ points for every text acronym or abbreviation," I say around a mouthful of pasta.

"This is why you haven't gotten laid in six months," Joel quips, still not looking up.

"Fuck you. It hasn't been that long."

Close.

I've been busy.

Busy sulking. First a soul crushing loss to end last season and then an injury that's kept me sidelined.

And I'm real tired of girls throwing themselves at me for the thrill of sleeping with a jock. Or in some sort of misplaced show of support to heal my fragile ego. Pity fuck? No thanks.

I know, I know. I got uptown problems.

"What happened to Sarah?" Nathan says as he stands and starts to jog in place.

"It was Tara, and last time I saw her, she was giving a big Valley welcome to a freshman soccer player."

Joel looks up. "God bless her dedication. She's single-handedly welcomed nearly every jock to campus in her short time here."

"Yeah, she's a real Mother Teresa." Z rolls his eyes. He's adamant about not messing around with girls in college so he can focus on ball and his quest to the NBA, so he thinks we're all petty assholes.

He isn't wrong.

An hour later, I'm in hell. Practice is shit. Shaw has talent, but he's all over the fucking place, trying to prove his worth by taking risky shots and hogging the ball. My nerves are shot. I can't do a damn thing but wait for this boot to come off.

"Reynolds, my office," Coach calls to the sideline when he's done giving orders for the guys to work on shooting drills.

I take my time, already knowing what he's going to say.

He's sitting behind his desk, and though I've seen him in his office before, it always strikes me how weird he looks perched upright like he's working a nine-to-five desk job. Some men just weren't meant for that kind of life, and coach falls squarely in that category. "Come on in, son. Have a seat."

I take the old chair in front of his desk. Thing looks like it's been here since the university opened in the fifties.

"How's the foot? Cast comes off in two weeks?"

"Yes, sir. I'm anxious to get back on the floor."

"And we're anxious to have you back, but the trainers say you may not be back fully for another two to four weeks after the boot comes off. We have the exhibition in two weeks and then our first game the week after. I know it isn't what you want, but have you considered a medical red shirt?"

I grind my back teeth to keep from speaking exactly what I'm thinking. Even knowing this was what he was going to say, it still pisses me off. Hell no, I don't want to redshirt my senior year. Sure, I take the redshirt and I'm still eligible to play an extra year. We get five years to play four seasons, but next year Z will be gone. I'll be done with my degree. It's an option. But it isn't one I'm willing to take.

"I'll be ready. Whatever it takes."

He nods. "Once you step out onto that floor, it gets a hell of a lot harder to take it back. You're sure about this? You can take some time and talk to your folks about it."

Right, like they give two shits about my ball career.

"Positive."

I can tell he's torn. He wants me to play and wants me to take the year to heal properly. I get it. I do. It's risky, but I'm prepared to do whatever it takes to be ready to go and to lead my team to a national championship. We were so close last year. Top four in the nation is good. Most people would be happy with that.

I'm not most people, and I want that national title.

5

BLAIR

Three more statistics classes pass in the same fashion. I sit, feverishly taking notes, as Wes sits in the back sleeping. Today I've given up the pretense of stellar note taking. My scribbles don't even make sense to me as I write them. It's more about keeping my hands busy and my attention trained forward.

I'm doodling hearts and flowers along the margin of my notepad when Professor O'Sean's monotone stops. The lack of noise is deafening.

"Mr. Reynolds," Professor O'Sean's voice booms off the walls of the room, and every person in the room, including me, duck and pray for invisibility to avoid being the next victim of public shaming in the form of being called on in class.

I keep my head low and peek up to the top row just in time to see Joel elbow Wes. Slowly, he lifts the hat and sits straighter.

"Mr. Reynolds, can you tell the class the probability of the example on the screen?"

I wince for him. Despite my glee that he's been caught sleeping, no one deserves to be grilled in front of the entire class.

"The probability is three-eights. It's a binomial distribution with a sample space size two to the third equaling eight. Would you like me to list the events?"

My mouth gapes. Wes wears an arrogant smile and boyish charm that makes the guys in class laugh and the girls swoon. Professor O'Sean has a begrudging look as he shakes his head to indicate the answer is sufficient. I'm inclined to be on his side. How dare Wes sleep through class and still know the answer? Here I am, taking notes and hanging on every word, and I still have no idea if I could have provided more to the answer than the scribblings I'd written down in my notes.

Glance at my neatly printed letters. The collection of all possible outcomes of an experiment is called a sample space. Yeah, that isn't helpful. All I've done is copy the definitions.

Without responding to Wes, Professor O'Sean moves on. At least I wasn't the only one who assumed the guy sleeping at the back of the class had no idea what was going on.

I dare another peek at the back row, stilling when I find Wes's gaze on me. He smirks as if mocking me instead of the teacher. My cheeks warm, and I turn quickly and keep my eyes forward for the rest of the class.

"There'll be another short test in two weeks that will cover the material in chapter three. The midterm is only one month away, and it makes up thirty-five percent of your overall grade. These tests are a taste of what will be on the midterm, so I suggest you prepare for them accordingly. Have a good weekend."

Good weekend? He's just ruined any possibility of my doing anything but studying from now until the test. I trudge up the stairs with a pit in my stomach, and a foreboding feeling that I'll be lucky to eke out a C in this class. So much for my stellar GPA and so much for getting into the highly competitive MBA program.

At the top of the stairs, I look up to see that Joel and Zeke wear worried expressions. Ones that I'm sure match my own.

Zeke scrubs a hand over his massive jaw. "Man, I don't think I can learn this shit by then."

Joel nudges him. "Sure you can. Wes could teach this stuff to children."

"Isn't that what I've been doing?" the man himself states dryly.

As I approach, he stands and meets me on the stairs.

"Blair." He says my name like a challenge.

"So, you're what some sort of statistics genius?"

"Your words."

"And in your words?"

"I already told you in my words, I could pass this class even if I never showed up." He shrugs as if it's no big damn deal.

I hold back an actual growl. "That's infuriating."

He grins wide. "And impressive?"

"Maybe, but more infuriating than impressive." I point toward his teammates. "And those two, *you're* tutoring them?"

"What? No, nothing like that."

Something tells me that's exactly what's happening. He looks almost embarrassed by the prospect. I don't know why it hadn't occurred to me before. I don't need to find a tutor; I've already found the best man for the job. I just have to convince him to help me.

The excitement of my idea must be written all over my face.

"Oh, no. No. I'm not a tutor."

"I know, but you obviously know your stuff."

"I'm sorry. I don't know the first thing about being a tutor, and even if I did, I don't have time. Between practice and homework . . ." He offers another shrug. "There's a reason I sleep in this class."

Nodding, I swallow the lump of disappointment in my throat.

I have no idea how I'm going to convince the statistics God to help me. I don't have anything to offer him. And my schedule is as insane as his until I get David off my back.

Between classes and practice, I don't doubt Wes is strapped for free time. And then there are the parties and the ladies. I'm no fool. I know how girls throw themselves at jocks. Vanessa's told me what it's like. She's ready to throw down every time a girl so much as looks at Mario. And they do a lot more than look.

So far, they seem to have gotten the memo V isn't one to mess with because I guarantee the first time one lays a finger on him—

innocent or not—she'll be walking around campus with a black eye or half her hair pulled out.

I digress . . . how do you get a man to do something he doesn't want to do for someone who insulted his intelligence and has absolutely nothing to offer him?

I mull over this question on the two-hour drive to Succulent Hill as I sing along to an old high school playlist. When I pull up to Gabby's house, I haven't managed to come up with any solutions, but I'm in better spirits anyway.

Gabby's mom, who had taken a job that allowed her to work from home after the accident, greets me at the door before I can ring the doorbell.

"Come in, honey. Gabby is upstairs." She rolls her eyes and shakes her head, smiling as if it were totally normal for her twenty-one-year-old daughter to be hiding away.

"Knock, knock," I call as I enter Gabby's room. Unsurprisingly, I find my best friend behind her laptop with eyes squinted behind thick glasses. My life has changed so much since the accident, I moved to Valley and did all the things we'd promised—pledge a sorority and major in business. I even force myself to go to Pilates occasionally.

I got my miracle that day. Whether it was thanks to God or the power of positive thinking, I'll never know for sure, but that day changed me forever.

Gabby's memory returned, but the fun-loving and determined girl I grew up with was lost during the crash. She stayed in Suck Hill, refusing to move away and basically hiding out in her parents' house. Deep down, her ambition hasn't changed. I know this because I almost always find her in front of her computer, studying or doing homework for her many online classes. She's a Valley U student, too, but taking classes online isn't the same as being on campus.

"Come in," she calls without looking up, and then as if just registering my voice, her eyes find mine and a big smile spreads across her face. "Blair."

I make the two-hour trip to Succulent Hill at least once a month to see Gabby and have dinner with my parents. Today, though, is just about Gabs.

"Happy birthday!" I squeeze her tightly and then step back to examine her outfit of yoga pants and tank. She looks fabulous, but she isn't exactly ready for dinner at our favorite local restaurant and pub. "You aren't ready."

She bites on her lip. "I thought maybe we could just hang out here."

"Uh-uh. You cannot celebrate your twenty-first birthday at home."

"But going out is so"—she sighs and then plops back down onto the bed—"soul crushing. I don't want to deal with the pity smiles or stares."

I try to see her as a stranger might. She has two long scars on the left side of her face that cross in an X. I think it makes her look badass, but I can't say I haven't noticed the looks she gets when we're in public.

"I promise to verbally attack anyone who dares to look at you the wrong way." She doesn't look convinced. "Come on, please?"

After a few more minutes of pleading, and twenty more minutes for her to change, Gabby and I head to dinner.

"How are classes going?" she asks as we're seated into a high-top table near the bar. She fidgets and keeps her gaze turned down, basically ducking out of anyone's line of vision.

"Mostly good. Statistics is a bit of a nightmare."

"You'll manage. You always do." Her voice is proud, almost motherly.

"I actually made quite an ass of myself trying to get a tutor," I admit. I like to fill her in on bits and pieces of college, but I almost always underplay the good and leave out the truly terrible—such as David blackmailing me. Somehow, it makes me feel less guilty about being the one pursuing our dream and hopeful that she might join me someday.

When I've finished telling her how I wrongly assumed Wes was a dumb jock, she is hysterical with laughter.

"It isn't funny," I say but join in laughing anyway. "I was a total ass, and now, I need to convince him to tutor me."

"You're going to have to grovel," she says decidedly. "Try food. Men love with their stomachs."

"I think that ship has sailed. I'll go with helpful acquaintanceship."

As she drinks her first legal adult beverage, I fill her in on Vanessa, who is always a favorite topic. Vanessa's life is way more entertaining than mine, and though, they've only met once, I think Gabby likes to hear our college escapades. And I'd never deny her that.

I've tried on more than one occasion to get Gabs to Valley, but she maintains she's perfectly content at home. I think she's hiding scared, but can I blame her? I'd like to think I'd be able to get out of bed each day and ignore the questioning looks, but I don't know if I'm that brave either. Still, I sometimes wish I could trade places with her. It's her dreams I'm living every day, and I can't help but think she deserves it so much more.

"Oh, hey, I made you a new bracelet to match mine." She lifts her arm and points to an orange bracelet. It's one of about twenty on her arm, but it matches the one she's slid to me across the table. "Another year of friendship."

I tie the bracelet around my wrist and then run a hand over my matching bracelets as I smile. "You know, Valley has a really great arts program, including jewelry and fashion design. You—"

"Not this again."

"Yes, this *again*. Gabby, you should be with me at Valley."

Before I can pitch her my best argument on all the reasons she should be at university, two guys approach our table.

They aren't bad-looking and are dressed as if they just came from work, but they look at least thirty-five. "Can we buy you ladies a drink?"

"Sure. Actually, it's Gabby's twenty-first birthday."

Gabby shifts, letting her hair fall over her face, and stares hard at the table top.

"Oh yeah? Happy birthday. Birthday shots are on us. What's your poison?"

It's silent for two long seconds before she looks up and meets his gaze. She flips her hair back, deliberately drawing attention to the scars. Both men drop their eyes.

"Fire ball," she says and finishes the drink in front of her in a long gulp.

"Coming right up." The men recover from their surprise and scurry off, presumably to get our drinks.

"*That* is why I can't go to Valley. I'd rather hide away in my parents' house than spend all day, every day, watching people react to my face."

"Ignore them. Those guys are idiots."

"It isn't just them," she insists. "Last week, a kid in the dentist waiting room cried when I sat beside him. He *cried*, Blair."

"Your scars are not that bad." I cringe at the way it sounds, but honestly, I don't see her the way she must see herself. She's still stunning. The scars didn't change her obvious beauty – only her confidence. "And anyway, college is different. I promise. No one cares. There's a guy in two of my classes who never wears shoes. He has these dirty, calloused feet, and he just owns it, and no one says a thing."

"Not to his face, just over drinks with friends."

The guys return, cutting our conversation short, and set four shots onto the table.

"What are we drinking to?" The guy closest to me asks.

I grab two shots, hand one to Gabby and lift the other in the air. "To Gabby. Happy twenty-first birthday to the most amazing chick I know. Love you, Gabs."

"Love you too," she says with a smile before we clink glasses and throw back the fiery cinnamon liquid.

Shortly after we've thanked them for the drinks, the guys seem to get the memo that we aren't interested and return to the bar.

Gabby and I sit and chat about anything and everything. With each glass we finish, Gabby acts more like the confident and happy girl of the pre-accident days.

"So, Vanessa is still dating the baseball guy, any prospects there for you?"

"I don't know," I admit. "I haven't met any of his teammates."

"Vanessa is dating a hot jock, and you haven't scoped out his friends? What's wrong with you?"

"I've been studying." I point a finger at myself. "Failing statistics a month into the semester."

"Lame. You need to get back out there." I resist the urge to throw the advice back at her. It's too good of a night to ruin.

But Gabby isn't done doling out the advice. "Seriously. You haven't dated anyone since David. What's up with that?"

"Nothing is up with that. I've just been busy."

She gives me a no nonsense look that has always caused me to cave under her peer pressure.

"All right fine. I'll scope out the hot baseball guys."

Satisfied, she smiles. "And report back."

6

BLAIR

I haven't seen much of Vanessa since she dropped statistics. She's taken to staying at Mario's most nights, and during the day, our class schedules keeps us out of sync. It goes without saying that when I find her rummaging through our closet singing along to K-pop the next night after work, I'm caught completely by surprise.

"What are you doing here? I thought you were staying at Mario's again tonight?" I ask as I set my backpack down at my desk. Four hours of working at the café has left me with sore feet and a kink in my neck. Not to mention, splattered with the sticky sweet syrups I can't seem to wash off my hands and always manage to smear in my hair.

And worst of all, my quotes went completely unappreciated tonight. I usually get at least one smile or thanks. So much for putting good out into the universe and getting it back.

"I am, *but* the guys are having an after-hours party and *you're* coming with me."

I attempt a smile that I'm sure looks more like a grimace. "Tonight? Shoot, you know I'd love to hang out, but I'm exhausted and have a class at eight tomorrow."

"Who signs up for eight a.m. classes past sophomore year?" She shakes her head. "And that was your excuse the last two weeks. You're coming."

"It was the only time advanced econ was available."

Vanessa pulls out a red tube top and shakes the hanger at me.

"No, not that one. Last time I wore it, I kept pulling it up all night afraid I was going to flash the entire bar."

"Would have made the night more interesting and maybe you wouldn't have ended up back here alone."

"How do you know I ended up alone that night?"

She raises two perfectly arched brows.

"Fine, I came home alone." It isn't that I'm a prude, but picking up a guy at a bar or party seems so freshman year. Is it too much to hope that a nice guy might notice me in the daylight, completely sober?

"Ever since that asshole David, you've been hiding away all this awesomeness." She waves a hand in front of me and waggles her eyebrows.

"I have a lot on my plate this semester." Vanessa doesn't know that my workload is double what it should be because David is blackmailing me into doing his work. I've considered telling her everything a million and one times, but I know Vanessa's reaction would be to march right over to his frat and kick him in the balls. It's exactly what I want to do every time I think about it, but I won't risk pissing him off and having him expose me in front of the entire college . . . or worse, wind up on one of those revenge porn sites.

I move past her, and I know I've already given in when I find myself scanning the clothes on my side of our tiny walk-in closet.

When we leave thirty minutes later, I've managed to shower and make myself presentable. I let Vanessa talk me into a short black dress that leaves none of my curves to the imagination, but I refused the high heels in favor of my chucks.

Vanessa has practically been living at the baseball house, and when we walk in, she's greeted enthusiastically. The two-story house is small, old, and borderline condemnable, but the upper classmen baseball players don't seem to care as they mill around.

The bars haven't closed yet, so the party is still small, mostly baseball players and their girlfriends and the many single girls vying for the guys' attention. A keg sits in the dining room, and an array of liquor bottles clutter the kitchen counters. Mario already has Vanessa's drink and is walking it over to her when we cross the living room.

"Hey, babe." He hands her the cup and drops a kiss to her temple. He puts an arm around Vanessa and addresses me. "What can I get you to drink?"

I don't even have to think about it. The smell of anything fruity or sweet makes my stomach roll after serving mochas and caramel macchiatos. "Vodka tonic. I don't suppose there's any lime in there?"

He shakes his head apologetically. "No tonic, either. How about Sprite?"

I nod my approval. I bet if Vanessa wanted tonic and limes he'd not only make sure there were limes but also he'd plant a tree out back.

"He is in love with you," I say when he disappears back into the kitchen.

A panicked look crosses Vanessa's face. "Don't be ridiculous. We've been dating for three weeks."

No one dates the first few months of a new school year. It's all the excitement of new students and different situations. Guys especially, but it isn't just them who reserve the first few months of the semester for hookups and having fun. I'd probably think he was in love with her regardless of the time of year by the way he caters to her every whim, but the fact that it isn't even October yet makes me certain.

Before I can detail out all the reasons why I believe it to be true, Mario is back with my drink.

"Thanks, Mario."

We stand, chatting and drinking, until the house begins to fill. Vanessa and Mario and two other couples claim spots on the couch, sitting on laps and watching the Phillies play the Diamondbacks. Neither being around happy couples or watching baseball are on my top one hundred ways to spend a Thursday night, so I venture downstairs where a makeshift DJ booth has been constructed from a card table and a sheet of plywood. The rest of the dingy unfinished basement has been cleared, and I find a few girls from my sorority holding red cups, shaking their butts, and singing way too loudly. The universal sorority girl version of dancing.

But I don't care that I can't dance for shit or that this basement smells of mold and cheap beer. For the first time all semester, I let it all go. All the worry about grades, David, Gabby . . . it's all pushed aside as I give in to the rhythm of the pop mix booming from two large speakers. This is what college is supposed to be—exhilarating situations without real-world stipulations. After we graduate, we won't be able to go out on a random Thursday night and let the night lead us wherever we want. We'll have jobs and careers to obsess over. Bills and responsibilities. With David on my ass, I've had a taste of what it might be like to have a prick boss breathing down my throat, and I'm not eager to enter that world yet.

"I need air," I yell over the music after the fifth song. Physical exertion has warmed my body and my soul. I move out of the circle, and the remaining girls close the space as I make my way up the stairs. I'm still moving to the beat of the music as I spot some of the basketball players, including Zeke and Joel. They stick out in this cramped stairwell, hunkering their tall frames down so they don't bang their heads on the ceiling.

Joel notices me first, and we pause on the stairwell, holding up traffic on both sides.

"Hey it's stat girl."

I chuckle at the nickname. It'll be flunked stat girl pretty soon if I don't pass this next test.

"What are you doing here?" I ask, genuinely surprised. I assumed the athletes didn't mix much outside of their own houses, and I can't remember ever bumping into any of the basketball team before. I'd like to think I wasn't so frat boy crazy that I wouldn't have noticed.

"Same thing you're doing here," he quips, and we both start to move on as the people behind us get impatient.

I look over the other guys and give them a brief nod. They're staring at me intently, and it's way too much attention for my poor underappreciated lady parts.

Mario and Vanessa are gone from their cozy spot in the living room, so I slip out the front door. The baseball house is sandwiched between two other houses, presumably for other sports teams. All the jocks live nearby, giving them close access to the training facilities across the street.

I follow the wrap-around porch to the side, hugging myself and enjoying the cool air whipping through my hair. September days in Arizona are still disgustingly hot, but the nights are the best. The sky is clear, and there is just a touch of heat in the air.

I inadvertently stumble upon a couple making out on the back side of the house, catching dark figures embraced so closely makes it hard to make out two distinct forms, but I see enough to know I should turn around and walk away. Reminders are everywhere I look that happy coupledom can exist in college. Or maybe it's just happy one-night stands. Honestly, I'm almost desperate enough to consider either as a step up from my current situation.

I quietly return to the front of the house, giving myself a silent pep talk to go in and have fun. Enjoy my carefree college years and ignore the stack of homework I need to finish. If only for one night.

"No way. *You're* at a dumb jock party?" Wes somehow manages to skip up the steps onto the porch.

Placing my hands on my hips, I give him a playful smile filled with attitude. "I never said all jocks were dumb."

"Just me."

Mario and Vanessa emerge from the shadows, looking rumpled and surprised to see people outside. That shock is quickly wiped away when Vanessa realizes it's just me and Mario calls out, "Wes, man, you made it."

They meet in the middle, slapping hands and doing that one-arm hug thing guys are so fond of.

"You two know each other?" Vanessa asks, stealing my thoughts.

The guys exchange a look that clearly says they think we are the idiots for not knowing they are friends.

"Wes is the only guy at Valley who spends more time at the fieldhouse than I do."

"Yeah, I'm gonna beat your deadlift weight just as soon as I get this thing off my foot," Wes says, nodding his head down to his booted leg.

"In the meantime, what do you say we get you a drink?"

The four of us make our way through the living room. Slowly. I hadn't thought of Wes as a big man on campus, but clearly, I missed the memo. Wes Reynolds – big damn deal.

As if my humiliation hadn't been bad enough before.

Guys yell out to him, slap his back, or ask about the foot. And the girls? If desperation has a smell, I am inhaling it now, and it reeks of flavored vodka and self-tanner. Hanging back, I glance around the room, paying particular attention to the way girls move so they'll be in his line of vision. Even the ones who aren't brave enough to come forward seem to be biding their time until he looks their way.

I grab Vanessa and pull her into the kitchen.

She careens her neck backward as if she can't bear to look away. "Did he get better looking since I dropped statistics, or have I been with one man for too long?"

I roll my eyes. "He puts me on edge. He has this arrogant charm that makes me want to kiss him and punch him at the same time. And I really need him to pass statistics, so I cannot make an ass of myself . . . again."

"Isn't it great? All that muscle and confidence and who would have guessed—brains!" Vanessa fills two cups with vodka and a splash of Sprite Zero and hands me one. "God bless smart jocks."

I play hide and seek with Wes for the rest of the night. To be fair, he has no idea we are playing any such game, but every time he comes into view, I duck out of the room. My theory is that if I don't talk to him, then I can't put my foot into my mouth. I still haven't figured out how I am going to convince him to tutor me, but I have a hunch that getting drunk and begging isn't the way.

Well after two in the morning, I drag myself outside and call the sober driver to take me home.

"You know, it seems you were practically invisible tonight." His voice sends goose bumps racing over my skin.

"Yeah, weird, I didn't see you either. Guess we just kept missing each other."

"You waiting for a ride?" He places both hands into his pockets, which forces me to really look at him. Dark jeans, a gray T-shirt that fits tight across his chest and arms, and tennis shoes . . . well, one tennis shoe.

The look suits him. I can't picture him in a dress shirt or loafers, my usual preference, but he works this look.

"Yeah, one of the girls should be here in a few minutes."

"One of the girls? Roommates?"

"Sort of. Sorority sisters. The sophomores take turns being sober drivers during the week."

"Smart idea."

"You guys don't have some sort of similar set up?"

"Nah. We can usually walk."

"Must be nice to be a guy sometimes and not have to worry about walking home alone in the dark."

He glances down at his body, pulls his hands from his pockets and runs one from his chest to his abs, which is where he lets it rest before pulling up the hem of his shirt just enough to tease me with the hard lines and a promise of a six pack. "I totally understand. I swear that every time I walk home, old ladies are honking and yelling out the window for me to take my shirt off or get in the car."

My mouth waters as I openly check him out. He's joking, but I have zero doubt that what he says is true.

He lets his shirt fall back into place. "Why don't you make the freshman do the sober driving?"

I shake my head and force my eyes back up to his face. "Excuse me?"

"Well, it makes more sense that you'd put that sort of crap job on the newest girls—sort of a rite of passage. I thought it was freshman who got hazed."

"Our freshman girls get the red carpet laid out for them. You don't gain loyalty and sisterhood by hazing."

"No?"

"People are more loyal when they respect and trust you. Respect and trust come from treating people well. A positive first year makes loyal sisters."

"Yeah, but if you put them through hell right away, then you know who will really be there when times get tough."

I consider this. "Fair point, I guess, but we aren't marching to war. Sisterhood is supposed to be fun."

"F-U-N," he says dryly.

The sober driver pulls up to the curb, and we say goodbye. As I walk away, I bite back the temptation to turn and ask him to reconsider being my tutor. I need to figure out what it is he wants or needs, and then I need to strike a deal.

7
BLAIR

I stop by the café before statistics Monday morning and then navigate to class carefully with a drink carrier full of coffees and a bag filled with muffins in my backpack. I'm running late thanks to the long line, but it works to my advantage when I spot Wes and crew already in their seats at the back of the auditorium.

"Good morning," I chirp.

"Stat girl," Joel calls out, giving me an easy smile.

Zeke nods, and Wes adjusts his hat just enough to reveal his eyes.

"Coffee?"

Joel and Zeke lunge for the drink carrier. Several girls sitting nearby flash me dirty looks, obviously thinking I've resorted to caffeine bribery to win them over, which is only partly true. They don't even look mad. They look more jealous that they didn't think of it first.

I pull my own drink free and then nudge the last coffee toward Wes. "Coffee?"

He eyes me warily but takes the drink.

"I have muffins too," I say conspiratorially as I take the seat in front of Wes and pull the brown paper bag from my backpack before handing it to an eager Joel. He and Zeke make quick work of the pastries. They don't offer any to Wes, and he doesn't even glance in their direction. He's laser focused on me.

"What are you up to, Blair?" he asks just as Professor O'Sean starts in on the lecture.

Shooting a playful smile, I swivel in my seat.

Halfway through the class, I turn my head slightly to get a glimpse of Wes, certain he'll be sleeping again, but I am surprised to find him staring at me. Our eyes lock, and I offer a small wave. He lifts a brow as if he's still trying to figure out my angle, but I just smile sweetly and return my focus back to the front.

When the class is over, I take my time packing my things.

Wes waits until the class has filed out and steps down a stair so he's very much in my way. "What's your play? Coffee and muffins just because?" He narrows his eyes.

"I work at the café on campus." I don't meet his gaze.

"You worked before class?"

Looking up hesitantly, I admit, "Well, no, but it was on my way."

Wes shakes his head. "Thanks for the coffee. I actually managed to stay awake for once."

He gives me a salute with his cup before he shuffles away.

"Wait," I call. Before his steely blue eyes have a chance to regard me in that arrogant, calculating way, the words spill from my lips. "One score makes happy *one* player. An assist makes two happy."

"Uhhh, what?"

"The quote on your coffee." I can feel my face warm and know I'm beet red. This is humiliating. Did I really use coffee and a cheesy basketball quote to win him over?

He lifts his fingers and turns the cup until he can read the words I scribbled.

I hang my head. Might as well go all in at this point. Too late to pretend this never happened. "I was wondering if you wanted to get together sometime this weekend to study? I can work around your schedule."

"Aww man, you mean I drank bribery coffee?" He looks down at the cup in his hand and curls his lip, eyes still smiling.

"Not bribery," I protest. "Friendship coffee. Come on, I need help. Just one time. Let me join you guys the next time you study, and I'll never bother you again."

It'll be easier to ask for more help once I've shown him what a quick learner I am.

Joel nudges him as he tips his head back finishing his coffee. When he's drunk every drop, he speaks, "You know Z and I are going to need to talk it out a bit more, let her join. Plus, girl used a Tony Kukoc quote. Mad props for that. Wait are you the café quote girl?"

I bite my lip and nod.

Wes shoots him a look to zip it, to which Joel just shrugs. Zeke just watches silently, but there's the slightest upturn to his lips.

"Fine. Be at the house at four this afternoon."

"Yes!" A victory smile breaks out on my face, and I don't even care if I look as ecstatic as I feel.

I hold on to those good feelings until I meet David at the library. He's disheveled, clothes wrinkled, hair mussed like he's been running his fingers through it. I hold back questions about how he's doing because, frankly, I don't care if he's having a rotten day.

"We had a pop quiz in computer programming," he says as I take the seat across from him.

It's the only class he didn't shove off on me because most of the work is done in class. You'd think he'd be able to manage one freaking class on his own, but apparently, he can't. I pass over the folder filled with the latest assignments he gave me without saying a word.

"I convinced Professor Reilly to let me do some extra credit to make up for the grade."

"Un-fucking-believable," I mutter as he hands me the paper with directions for the additional work. "I don't know shit about programming, David."

His lip twitches on one side, and he takes out a heavy textbook and plops it down between us. "Thought you'd say that."

I'm still staring at it baffled when he stands. "Need it by Tuesday next week."

Awesome. Add programming to my list of classes this semester, why the hell not?

I read the directions five times. Yep, five. I give up and shove it in my bag. I'll deal with it this weekend.

My shift at the café ends at three thirty, so I reek of coffee and whipped cream as I walk up the sidewalk toward a house I can't believe belongs to anyone I know.

It's only a block from the baseball house so I guess it's fitting – most the jocks live near the fieldhouse. But this isn't like any other off campus house I've seen. It's huge, and the lawn is manicured with shrubbery and flowers. It's obviously landscaped professionally and often.

I check the address three times. It's only when I hear the faint sound of a basketball bouncing from inside that I believe I'm in the right spot.

Wes's instructions were not to knock, so I disregard all manners and push open the door and hold my breath, preparing for anything.

Standing in the entryway of the massive place, I gawk. The room I share with Vanessa would fit inside the foyer.

Zeke comes down the stairs, sans shirt, a pair of long shorts slung low on his hips. I try not to stare but I figure it would be a crime not to admire all that muscle. A series of tattoos trail from his left shoulder all the way down to his fingers. He nods to me and attempts a small smile. His gesture makes me take a deep breath and relax.

"Hey, Zeke," I pause. "You know where I can find Wes?"

"He's in the gym upstairs."

"The gym . . ." My voice trails off as he continues past me walking toward an open room with a large television mounted on the wall. Unsurprisingly, it's tuned to ESPN and a couple of guys are lounged back in big armchairs that look like theater seating.

"You aren't coming?" I call after him. Joel mentioned they'd need help too.

He shakes his head and keeps going without saying any more.

Oh-kay. I walk up the stairs, the sound of basketballs leading me to the court. It's a half-sized version of the one at Ray Fieldhouse and even has the roadrunner mascot painted on the sideline.

Three guys are positioned around the hoop, a ball cart full of basketballs between them, but Joel and Wes huddle together on one side. A shirtless Joel stands with his hands on his hips, watching Wes carefully. Wes has a basketball in one hand and uses his other to emphasize whatever he's saying.

I walk slowly toward them as I take in Wes's focused and determined face and the way he so effortlessly holds the ball, dribbling it occasionally or palming it with one large hand, fingers splayed out to cover what seems like half the ball. It doesn't look like he is even aware he is doing it. The ball is an extension of his hand.

Joel nods slowly, as if a light bulb is being switched on in that pretty head of black hair. He holds both hands out, asking for the ball as he cuts to the top of the three-point line. Wes passes, a crisp fast move that has the ball in Joel's hands before I can be thoroughly impressed with the way he moves. The ball arches to the net and in. The guys move toward each other happy smiles on both their faces as they exchange some words I can't quite hear.

"Hey." I hang back a few feet, giving them room for their bro moment.

Joel and Wes turn to me in unison.

"Stat girl," Joel says with a smirk. "You're just in time. We're just finishing our study session. He's all yours."

Joel has the sort of charisma and good looks that convince girls to do dumb things like make out with their friends or follow him to his room.

Or send nude photos.

I shake away the negativity and give his sweaty forehead and chest a once over. It doesn't look like much studying has taken place, but I'm not about to argue that point.

Joel lifts his head to Wes in acknowledgment. "Thanks, man." He bounces the ball to Wes and tips his head to me. "Catch you later."

"It's just the two of us?" My voice is a screech, but I'm too nervous to care. "I thought Zeke and Joel were joining us."

"They had some stuff they needed to do this afternoon, so we studied early. They're good, so that just leaves you."

We stare at each other for a moment. Well, I stare. He is probably trying to figure out what is wrong with me while simultaneously devising a plan to get the crazy, gawking girl away from him. He has to be used to that by now, though, right?

"You ready?" Wes finally asks.

"Sure. Yep. Great," I manage with more confidence than I feel.

"We can study downstairs in the television room, but I think some of the guys are down there hanging out, or we could go to my room."

"Your room," I blurt too quickly and then fumble to cover my slip. Great, now I sound like I just want to get him alone. "I mean, the quiet would be good."

"Cool." He motions for me to go before him, and I backtrack out of the gym and into the hallway.

"This way."

I let him take over, and I follow him past open bedrooms while I openly admire the living arrangements these guys have. I've counted three bedrooms already. Each one is large and set up almost in a dorm format with the same bed frame, desk, and large flat screen mounted on light yellow walls. And the bedding and décor isn't bachelor style mismatch stuff picked up from Target. It's all in team colors, and the roadrunner mascot makes an appearance in much of it.

"This is me."

His room looks exactly like the others, but I still scan it from floor to ceiling, looking for clues that make it different. Make it solely his.

"This is your room?" I turn and grin. "What no balcony or bathroom?" I say sarcastically.

"Joel has the master since his dad paid for the house."

My attention snaps to Wes, and the wheels turn as I piece together what I've read about the team and his last name clicks. It should have since it's plastered all over campus. "Joel Moreno. He's a Moreno, like, Moreno Hall and—"

"The president of Valley University? Yup."

Wes grabs the statistics book and a pair of glasses from his desk before taking a seat on his bed.

"Chair's yours if you want it, or you can sit up here. Big bed." He slides his glasses on and then flips open the book, and I swear it's like someone turns on a wind machine. The black rimmed glasses take him from hot jock to hot *smart* jock, and I know this must be what it's like for guys watching a supermodel eat a double cheeseburger. It seems all wrong, and yet, it is sooo right.

"You have specific things you want to go over? Questions? I'm not a tutor, so I don't really know the right way to do this."

I take a seat on the edge of the bed. My heart rate spikes just being this close to him. "Joel and Zeke seem confident enough so whatever you taught them in the past few hours seem to contradict your modesty."

He scrubs a hand over his jaw. "Yeah, all right. How about we start with measuring variation in data sets?"

For the next thirty minutes, Wes basically recites the book as I ask questions and pour over the notes I've taken in class. He never looks at the book before he answers. He flips through it a few times when I mention something in reference to a chapter number, but he seems to be an encyclopedia.

His effectiveness, though ... I mean, I have read the book on my own, but I'm not even remotely close to understanding a fraction of what he does.

Zeke walks in and then freezes. "Sorry, didn't realize you two were still studying. Practice in ten."

Wes takes off the glasses and sits back on the bed, resting his large frame against the wall. He clears his throat like all the talking has made him lose his voice. I suppose lecturing to a person for an hour could do that.

I gather my notes and shove everything into my back pack as I try to lift the fog that has settled over my brain. This is worse than the confused and drugged feeling I have when I leave Professor O'Sean's class. I'm more confused than ever. Between the glasses and his general hotness, I barely registered a word he said.

When someone likes the way a person's voice sounds, they often say they could listen to them read the phone book. Yeah, that's basically what just happened. He read me the stat book and his smooth voice and handsome face mesmerized me, but I learned absolutely nothing.

I stand and shift toward the door. "Thank you for the, umm . . . help. See you guys on Monday."

Wes follows me to the door with a scowl on his face. "Sure. No problem. Hope you got what you needed. I'm sorry to cut out, we have late practice tonight."

"Practice on Friday nights, huh?"

"Every day. We have an exhibition game coming up."

I nod and shift one foot farther as I consider asking if I can come back for more help just to see him put the glasses back on. It wouldn't help my grade, but it'd certainly brighten the day. "Thank you again."

I spend the rest of Friday night finishing David's music appreciation paper and Saturday alternating between trying to figure out this stupid computer programming assignment, trying to study for statistics, and figuring out what I'm going to do when I fail the midterm and have to drop the class with an incomplete. I'm taking four classes this semester. That isn't counting the four classes David is enrolled in but passing along to me. I'm drowning in assigned reading, research, and assignments.

As the quiet sorority house starts to buzz with excitement of girls getting ready for a Saturday night out, I finally give up any pretense of absorbing any more information.

With no other plans for the night, I find myself back at the baseball house. I shoot Gabby a text to let her know I'm back and scoping out the hot jocks. She replies with about ten smiley faces. I'm standing with Vanessa, Mario, and a freshman named Clark, who hasn't left my side since I walked through the door unattached. He's funny, charming, and cute, but I have one eye aimed on the door as he trails on about his first months in the Arizona heat. And if my pulse accelerates at the sight of Joel and Zeke entering the party . . . well, I'll blame that on the alcohol and not the blip of hope that another player might not be far behind.

"I didn't realize the baseball team was tight with the basketball team," I say to Mario and Clark, trying for nonchalance. "Aren't you guys supposed to have some sort of rivalry or something over gym time and national titles?"

Clark pipes in. "Basketball team is cool. It's the soccer guys we don't like."

Mario gives Clark a glare. "We don't have beef with any of the jocks."

A steady stream of guys I now recognize as basketball players follow in behind Joel and Z. It looks like the whole team is here . . . sans one. Maybe Wes is busy memorizing more of the statistics book. How does someone get that sort of knowledge? I consider myself bright, but he has some sort of effortless genius. Or it appears effortless anyway.

I wave to Joel and Zeke as they look out over the crowd but resist the urge to go hang out with them and ask where Wes is. Maybe he's just late like last time. I don't know why I'm hoping for the latter, but as I let Clark attempt to dazzle me with more conversation, my nerves start to fray a bit more each time the front door opens.

"Listen to me go on and on, tell me about you, Claire."

His inability to even remember my name annoys me and snaps

me out of my trance. "You know what? I think I'm gonna go home and study. I'm failing statistics, and I'm stressing and ... well, I won't bore you."

I turn without waiting for his reply and curse the heels that are pinching my feet with every step. I knew I should have stuck with my guns and worn my chucks, which make much better getaway shoes.

"Wait, can I get your number?" I hear him call but hurry my pace and don't stop until I'm a block away and it's clear Clark has given up the chase. I laugh to myself. Did I really think a guy who couldn't even remember my name was going to follow me to get my number?

I keep walking, waiting to call a sober driver, telling myself it's because it's still early and it is a nice night to walk a bit, but when I arrive at the front of Wes's house, I stop and look up at it for signs that he's inside. The faint sound of a basketball being dribbled catches my attention, and I smile, imagining Wes inside hard at practice. Maybe it isn't even him, he has another roommate I haven't met, and Wes did mention that all the guys on the team hung out here. Still, I want to imagine it's him practicing and that's what kept him from a night out with his friends.

I take another step down the sidewalk and pull out my phone to dial the sober driver when I realize the sound I'm hearing is outside. It's the echo of a basketball hitting pavement and not the gym floor inside. Curious, I ignore every single girl horror story thing I've learned about trespassing and being out alone at night and I walk toward the noise. The parking garage for the house curves around the back, and in the far corner, they have a basketball hoop set up. The rusted backboard and chain look out of place with the immaculate house. It's funny to me that anyone would be out here playing when they have such a nice court inside.

In the darkness, I can't make out his face, but the movements are all him. Even without the cast, I think I would be able to pick him out of a silhouette lineup of athletes.

I cross the lot, taking advantage of the view. He's tossed his shirt on the ground and wears a pair of athletic pants that zip at the ankles but are open on the right leg around his cast. The late summer night has cooled, but sweat beads up and shines in the light the streetlights cast around him.

"Hey, Reynolds. Didn't anyone tell you it's Saturday night?"

He stops under the hoop, but he doesn't stop dribbling as he stands to his full height. "Best time to be out here. Got the whole court to myself."

"And no spectators to appreciate the view."

"If you build it, they will come..."

"How's that?"

He palms the ball and extends his arm toward me. "You're here."

"I'm not much of a spectator." I close the distance between us and take the ball from him. I turn the ball over in my hands and then dribble it twice, hyper aware that he is watching me. I stop a couple of feet in front of the hoop and shoot the ball.

"Yes!" I call out when the ball rattles around the rim and goes through the net.

"Nice shot." He catches the ball and passes it back to me. I shoot it again, but the basketball gods are fickle, and it bounces off the rim.

"Try again."

He passes it back to me, and I take my time lining up and concentrating at the free throw line. The ball sails up, and I hold my breath until it swishes through the net. Gabby and I played one whole year of junior varsity basketball before we determined we were not cut out for competitive sports.

"Two out of three. You have a spot for me on the team?"

"Sixty-six percent would have you riding the pine."

"What about you? You gonna be ready to play this season?"

He looks down to the cast and grimaces. "Comes off next week, but I won't know what sort of shape I'll be in until then."

"What'd you do? If you don't mind my asking."

"I don't mind," he says and dribbles the ball slowly. "Stress fracture. I hurt it in practice about a month back. Just came down on it wrong and that was it."

"I broke my arm once. Missy Thomas pushed me off my bike. My cast was pink, though."

He looks down at his black cast and then pushes his bottom lip out in a pout. "They didn't give me that option."

"Too bad."

He tosses the ball to me almost as if he's forgotten I'm me and not one of his teammates.

"So, really, why are you out here on a Saturday night and not out with the guys? I saw Joel and Z and a bunch more of your teammates at the baseball house. Were you busy memorizing more textbooks?"

He arches a brow.

"I took a guess. The way you know statistics, I assumed you spent your spare time memorizing it."

He chuckles. "Photographic memory. Plus, statistics is my life."

"How do you mean?"

"Well, say I get fouled taking a shot and get two free throws. Each shot has two outcomes: make or miss. So, there are four possible outcomes. I could miss both shots. Miss the first shot and make the second. Make the first and miss the second."

"Or make both."

He grins. "Exactly."

I stare at him as he moves around the court, and I process what he just told me. "Oh my God. This is how you've been tutoring Joel and Z."

He shrugs. "Not tutoring, just explaining it in terms they understand. They're smart dudes, but ball is our life. So, by giving them examples about shit that doesn't mean anything to them is a lost cause."

"Wes, that's genius. Can you show me more? Explain it like you've been doing for Joel and Z?"

Scrubbing his hand over his jaw, he studies me carefully. "I don't know how much sense I'm going to make talking ball stuff with a chick in a dress and heels."

"Don't let the outfit fool you. I can keep up."

"That so?"

"Yep. I'm not some prissy sorority girl."

He gives me a once over that sends a shiver through me.

"Okay, well, I am, but it isn't *all* I am. I've played basketball before."

"Yeah, how long ago was that?"

"It was a while ago," I admit. "Come on, please?"

"The sorority girl wants the dumb jock to tutor her? It's pretty funny, really."

"Sorry I assumed you were a dumb jock."

"You're only sorry because you need my help."

"I'll play you for it."

"Play me for what exactly?" He cocks his head to the side.

"More of your tutoring services."

"You think *you* can beat *me*??" He raises a brow as he spins the ball around in his hand. He's showing off, but I'm very much enjoying it.

"Not one-on-one." I hold my hands out, and he bounces it to me. I moved to the side of the basket, dribble once and pull up and shoot. As the ball goes through the net, I turn to him. "We'll play PIG."

One side of his mouth tugs into a half smile, but he retrieves the ball and dribbles it to where I stand. I hold my spot, so he moves behind me, the warmth from his body swallowing me up. He leans down so that his lips are a hair's breath away from my neck. "I'm seventy-five percent from the left wing. You sure this is your play?"

I turn my head to meet the arrogant glint in his eye and nod. "I'm not intimidated."

That's a lie, but I'm not about to show any more weakness in front of this guy.

Without taking his eyes from mine, he raises the ball over my head and shoots. The sound of the ball swishing through the net is the only indication it went in. That, and the swagger and cocky athleticism that ooze from him as he retrieves the ball.

And so it goes. I take shot after shot, taking my time and concentrating like I haven't since the SATs, and then he makes the shot while watching me. It's infuriating. And seriously hot.

When I miss, he takes over, picking spots all over the court and moving back a foot each time. Miraculously, I manage to capitalize twice, and we're tied, both having P-I.

"Only one more letter."

"Don't count your chickens before they're hatched." Lining up at the free throw line, I turn away from the basket and hold the ball with two hands. I hear him snicker, but I keep focused on the shot. Trying not to overthink it, I toss it up and over my head and then crane my neck around to watch as it rattles through the net.

"You got trick shots," he says, sounding more impressed than anything.

"Trick shots? Does it somehow count less this way?"

He chuckles and shakes his head. "Fair enough."

He lines up in my spot, peeking over his shoulder once before facing away from the basket and tossing the ball up into the air. The ball hits the front of the rim and bounces back to him.

"Yes! I did it! I beat the conference assist leader."

"Seems you do know my stats."

Heat floods my cheeks. "I might have looked you up. I won! I won!"

"You got lucky. I demand a re-match."

"Nope. I won fair and square." I walk off, grabbing my purse and phone from where I left them.

"You're leaving?"

"I know when it's time to walk away. Tomorrow at two work?"

I don't look back, but I can feel him smiling after me. "See ya then, baller."

THANKS FOR READING this sample of The Assist. This book continues to be one of the favorites I've written!

All the books in the series can be read as a standalone, but here's the reading order.

The Assist
The Fadeaway
The Tip-Off
The Fake

SECRET PUCK

CAMPUS NIGHTS BOOK ONE

Secretly hooking up with the team captain's sister was a bad idea.
In my defense, the first time I saw her I didn't know who she was. Kind, gorgeous, a little naïve. Ginny brightened my world from day one.
I knew I was no good for her. She was just out of a relationship and I had a reputation for having a new girl in my bed every weekend. I tried to do the right thing. Honest.
I'm the one who insisted we should be just friends.
That lasted about as long as you'd expect.
But Ginny? She's the best—best friend, best everything.
So yeah, hooking up with the team captain's sister wasn't a great idea.
Would I do it again?
In a heartbeat.

1

GINNY

August

"What are you doing here?" I ask my brother through a small crack in the door.

He leans his large frame against it, widening the gap and keeping me from closing it on him. "I'm checking on my favorite sister."

"I'm your only sister."

He pushes a big shoulder against it, and I give up on trying to keep him out. Crossing the small dorm room in three steps, I resume my position on the bed.

"Have you left the dorm at all this weekend?" He follows me and takes a seat at the end of my bed. "Hey, Ava."

My roommate Ava's on the phone with her boyfriend Trent, but waves and blushes when Adam acknowledges her.

"I'm enjoying my last days of summer vacation," I tell him as I pull my hair down from the messy bun and attempt to make it look like I haven't been rocking this same hairstyle for three days. It's the day before classes start and the only things going on around campus are parties and new student activities—neither of which have sounded appealing enough to get dressed and leave my room.

He picks up the package of cheese and peanut butter crackers I'd been devouring when he knocked. "This looks like the opposite of fun. And you bailed on my party last night."

"A party with a bunch of your teammates... yeah, no thanks."

"You can't sit in here moping forever. Bryan did you a favor. Long-distance relationships in college suck. Next to no one survives them. Plus, the guy was a tool anyway. Don't let it ruin college. College is awesome."

My heart cracks a little more at the reminder that my ex-boyfriend, who should be with me at Valley starting our freshman year together, decided at the last minute to go to Idaho instead.

It wasn't entirely his fault. He got the offer after they'd lost their second-string quarterback to an injury. Bryan became their new second-string and I was cut from his roster altogether.

Adam nudges my arm with his elbow. "Come on. Let's grab lunch, or come over and hang at the apartment, meet my roommates. *You don't need no man. There's plenty of fish in the sea.* What kind of pep talk are you feeling?"

I smile. "Of course you think there's plenty of fish in the sea. You have a new girlfriend every semester."

"Exactly. I speak from experience."

I don't think it'll be that easy for me. My brother is a hockey player, tall and muscular, and I guess objectively he's attractive. He certainly has no problem finding girlfriends if that's any indication. He has perfect hair; I'll give him that. I've had hair envy my whole life. Where my dirty blonde hair is stuck somewhere between straight and curly, his is lighter, thick, and the longish strands hang perfectly at the nape of his neck.

"How about lunch?" he asks.

It's tempting, really. If anyone can make me feel better, it's Adam, but I'm not sure I want to feel better yet.

Being single is a wonderful and liberating thing. "Single and ready to mingle." "I'm every woman." "Put your hands up." "Truth hurts". There are so many songs about it, I can't even list them all. But the thing about the single girl anthem... it's usually born out of a lot of tears from the last heartbreak.

The girl power and celebration of singledom only comes after you've cried your eyes out and burned every item that belonged to the last man who did you wrong.

I'm still somewhere between the two, but I catch Adam's drift—it's probably time to re-enter the land of the living.

I let out a cleansing sigh. "Tomorrow. Breakfast tomorrow, I promise. I need to help Ava get our room organized." I glance over to the boxes stacked on top of my desk that I still haven't unpacked.

Adam doesn't look convinced.

"I said I promise."

He holds his pinky out and I roll my eyes but link it with mine.

"I'll swing by on my way to the dining hall. You've got an eight o'clock, yeah?"

I nod and groan. I am so not a morning person. "Yeah, but you don't."

"Preseason workouts this week and next at six. I'll be heading over to eat around that time anyway."

"Six o'clock in the morning?"

"Yeah. In the morning." The deep chuckle that follows makes me smile. He stands and ruffles my already messy hair.

"Stop it." I swat at his hand. He knows I hate it when he treats me like I'm twelve. In his mind, a three-year age gap makes him *so* much wiser.

"Be ready at quarter `til," he says as he moves to the door. "I'd hate to have to bang on the door and wake up the entire hall."

"God, you're obnoxious," I say, but he's already gone.

I get up and shower, hoping it washes away some of the lingering sadness along with the cracker crumbs. Back in my room, I look around it with fresh eyes and cringe. Ava's side is organized and decorated with bright colors and then there's my side. Even I can admit it looks a little depressing. Okay, a lot. White concrete walls, gray bed frame, and desk. The only color is my pale-yellow comforter.

After I'm dressed, I finally unpack. I didn't bring a lot of personal items because so many of them reminded me of Bryan. I fill the closet with my clothes and shoes, organize all of my school stuff on the desk, and I tape up a few pictures of my family and friends from high school on the wall.

Standing back, I survey the results. It's a start, and I feel a little more ready to face the world tomorrow. I flip on the small bedside light and crawl under the covers to sleep. I pick up my phone out of habit. Nothing good ever happens from scrolling your phone after midnight.

All of my friends from high school are posting selfies and tours of their new college dorms. There's Bryan, handsome as ever, in blue and orange. The college campus is in the background and he's lined up beside a group of big guys I assume are other football players based on their size. They hold beers and smile looking at the camera. He's obviously having no problem enjoying college without me.

That same handsome face I've known my whole life. We were neighbors, childhood friends, and then high school sweethearts. I close my eyes and the last conversation I had with him replays in my mind.

"I don't understand. What do you mean you're not going to Valley? We're supposed to leave in three days." We lie on my bed and I'm still in that post-sex high, so it takes me a few seconds to realize he's serious.

His heavy weight on top of me suddenly feels claustrophobic. "I got a call from the coach at Boise State. One of their incoming freshmen got into a car accident. He's out all year, maybe longer."

"But we've been planning on going to college together for two years, and Idaho is like... a long way from Arizona. How is this going to work?"

He hesitates and runs a hand over his jaw while he studies me with an embarrassed look on his face.

"Oh my god. You're not just telling me you're going to Boise; you're ending this?" I motion between us.

"I don't think it would be fair to either of us to go to college with unrealistic expectations. You said it yourself, Idaho is a long way from Arizona. When we come back for holidays or summer vacations, we can pick up where we left off. You'll always be my perfect girl, Ginny." His gaze drops from my face to my cleavage and continues doing a long sweep of my naked body. The least a guy can do is avoid staring at your boobs while he breaks up with you. Or pull out. *"But, I think we should give ourselves the freedom to explore and have fun while we're apart."*

"Why would you break up with the perfect girl? That doesn't make any sense," I mutter quietly to the room, swiping a rogue tear. I didn't give him the satisfaction of seeing me cry then and I'm not going to let him ruin my first day of college tomorrow.

I force a smile as I reimagine all the amazing things college will bring without Bryan. For starters, I don't have to do anything I don't want to. I can be absolutely selfish with my time. Truthfully, I have no idea what that looks like anymore, but I'm ready to find out.

I put in my earbuds, hit play, and fall asleep with Beyoncé on repeat.

―――

THE NEXT MORNING, Ava and I get ready for classes. She's got the TV hooked up and *Vampire Diaries* season one, episode one playing. Feels right somehow. The first season of everything starting today.

Our room finally looks like two excited freshmen live here. Ava's side is a little more personalized, photos of her and Trent, her boyfriend, take up most of the wall above her bed.

My roommate is in a serious relationship with her high school boyfriend, who is going to college upstate. It was something else we'd shared when we first connected over the summer, being in serious relationships. They don't seem concerned about the distance, although it's not nearly as far as Idaho.

Ava's been on the phone or texting him the better part of the last week since we moved in. She's nice and I think we'll be great roommates. I guess since she's in a relationship, at least I won't have to worry about her bringing random guys back to the dorm. Because I'll be starting college single and not exactly thrilled about the opposite sex, it'll be nice not to worry about that.

"Do you want to come to breakfast with us?" I ask as I'm preparing to leave.

"No thanks." She shakes her head, making her short, black hair toss around her heart-shaped face. "I'm going to video chat with Trent on our way to our first classes."

A little pang of jealousy hits me, but I push it aside and head downstairs to meet Adam. Excited energy floats in the air. Blue and yellow banners hang on the front of the dorms welcoming us to the new school year.

Students are already out in droves heading off to classes, backpacks strapped to their shoulders, coffees in hand. They walk mostly in groups to their destinations; those who don't have earbuds in or stare down at their phones.

The Valley campus is truly beautiful. When we dropped Adam off before his freshman year and I got a look at the campus for the first time, I knew that it's where I wanted to go to college too. The buildings are mostly old and historic looking, green grass makes it feel a little less like the desert, and there's a huge fountain in the middle of campus.

"Ginny," Adam calls out, catching me by surprise while I'm lost people watching.

"Hey." I turn to see him and his friend and teammate Rhett with him.

"You remember Rauthruss?" Adam asks and runs a hand through his still-damp hair. Even wet it looks better than mine.

Rhett grins and steps forward with his hands shoved in his pockets. "Hey, Ginny. Good to see you again. Welcome to Valley."

Rhett Rauthruss is a giant man-boy. He's tall and built. His legs are like tree trunks. Seriously, his thighs could crush my head. But he's got this baby face and pouty mouth that keeps him from looking too intimidating. He's also got a really great Minnesota accent that I absolutely love.

He and Adam have been teammates and roommates since their freshmen year, so I've met him a few times over the years and he came home with Adam once last semester for a weekend.

"Hey, Rhett, good to see you too."

He grins a little shyly.

"Are we ready?" Adam asks. "I'm starving."

My dorm doesn't have its own dining hall, so we cross the street to Freddy Dorm to eat. I follow Adam and Rhett inside, and we fall into the long line of people entering the dining hall, scanning their student ID cards as they go.

The smell of burned toast hangs in the air as we shuffle inside the busy dining room. Rhett heads off at a near jog for food, but Adam hangs back with me. "Grab food and then meet us at the big table in the right corner. You can't miss us."

With that, he rushes off too.

I do a lap while I check out the food options. Five or six different stations are set up with varying breakfast foods ranging from yogurt to omelets and everything in between.

I decide on waffles, get at the end of the line, and pick up a tray. The guy in front of me drums his fingers on the back of his tray impatiently. His fingers are long and strong-looking… somehow just really attractive. I let my gaze move up to his forearms and appreciate them in the same way. Tan and toned. The gray T-shirt he's wearing hugs his back and the short sleeves are snug against his biceps. Muscular but not too beefy.

When it's finally his turn, he sets the tray down and grabs a plate. With his profile to me, I take in his straight nose and sharp cheekbones. Dark, messy hair that I have the ridiculous urge to run my fingers through, sticks up on his head.

I think maybe I spent too many days in my dorm room crying over Bryan. I'm flat out gawking at this point, but it's a little hard not to. This guy is attractive without even getting a front view. He has this whole look about him that feels like he didn't bother glancing in the mirror this morning. Actually now that I think about it, it's a little frustrating that I spent twenty minutes taming my hair while he rolled out of bed and managed to look like that.

Damn. Welcome to Valley, Ginny.

He proceeds to fill his plate with four waffles. These aren't the size of the small, frozen waffles that you pop in the toaster, they are huge, bigger than my head waffles. He grabs a second plate and fills that one with bacon and eggs farther down the line. He glances between his plates and the food still left on the warmers ahead like he might not be finished.

I chuckle and he glances back at me. My breath hitches when his blue eyes meet mine. Not blue, a thousand shades of blue. He gives me a sheepish smile.

"Can you hand me another plate?" His deep voice washes over me, vibrating my insides. He's a lot to take in, but I do, not able to stop myself. His hair isn't only dark brown, it has hints of lighter strands too. It's like no part of him could decide on being one thing and instead he's made up of varying shades and depths.

He has an athletic build, tall but not towering over me like Bryan did. My ex was six foot four, which made him a great height to see over a mass of bodies on the football field, but not so great for kissing without standing on my tiptoes. I'm standing here wondering if I could kiss this guy flat-footed.

Aaand he asked me a question.

"Are you serious?"

He doesn't bat an eye, so I grab another plate and hand it to him.

"Thanks."

I fill my plate with one waffle like a reasonable human and continue to scoot down the line behind him. He's added four pieces of toast and a handful of grape jelly packets to the third plate, and he's *still* eyeing the food ahead of us.

"Are you feeding a family of bears?"

One side of his mouth pulls up. "Just one very hungry dude."

We reach the end of the line and he slows like he's waiting for me. He eyes my tray. "Barely four hundred calories on that plate. How are you going to make it to lunch?"

"Somehow I think I'll manage."

We start walking, both in the same direction.

"Are you following me?" I ask when we've walked shoulder to shoulder for three steps.

"No. I think you're following me." We reach the table where Adam and Rhett are seated with a group of guys.

"Yo, Heath!" one of the guys calls to him.

It takes a couple of seconds for my brain to catch up.

"You're a hockey player?" I frown while I try to place him. I've only met a few of Adam's teammates, but I've been to several games, so I'm surprised I don't recognize him.

His brows pull together studying me, maybe trying to place me as well. "Not a fan of hockey? I think you're at the wrong table then."

Adam stands and puts a protective arm around my shoulders. "She's not a fan of any men at the moment."

Kill me now.

I stare down at my white tennis shoes as Adam introduces me. "Guys, this is my baby sister, Ginny. It's her first day."

The group offers their hellos and grunts of acknowledgment. They've all got several plates of food in front of them like Heath and are shoveling it in like they haven't eaten in days.

I take a seat and so does Heath, across from me.

"Did you come to the games last year?" he asks as he pours syrup over his waffles.

"Yeah, a couple. Why?"

"I don't recall seeing you."

This makes me laugh. In a crowd of cheering fans, how could he possibly remember? "I don't recall seeing you either."

He leans across the table with a cocky smirk. "I was the one doing all the scoring."

2

GINNY

I EAT MY BREAKFAST, staying mostly quiet while the guys talk back and forth. They complain about the workout this morning and talk up the season. I've gotten good over the years at tuning out hockey talk.

I catch Heath staring at me an uncomfortable number of times. Uncomfortable because I only know he's staring at me because I'm staring at him too.

Oh, and he eats every one of the giant waffles, plus the rest of his food.

"Where's your first class?" Adam asks me as we're finishing up.

"Umm... the humanities building, I think."

He nods and sits back in his chair. "You know where it's at? Want me to walk you?"

I resist rolling my eyes. "Yes. I'll be fine."

"Humanities building?" Heath asks. "I'm walking that way."

Standing, I put on my backpack and then pick up my tray. "I've got it, really." I glance at my brother. "See you later." And then I give a little wave with my free hand to the rest of the table.

As I'm dropping my empty tray, Heath steps up beside me. "Adam Scott's sister... I don't see the resemblance."

"Thank you... I think?"

He's still following me when we get to the exit. "There's really no need. I know where I'm going."

"Okay." He shrugs one shoulder. "See you around, Ginny Scott."

The way he says my name is taunting and playful and has my tummy doing weird, excited things.

"Hopefully not if I want there to be any food left to eat," I say before he can leave.

I should walk away now, but there's a bizarre chemistry between us and something about him makes me feel the best I have in days. We stand a foot apart, grinning at one another and forcing people to go around us.

He snaps out of it first. "Better get here early for lunch then. That's when I get in my big meal for the day."

"Your big meal?" I can't help but laugh.

"That was nothing. I burned those calories before you woke up this morning."

"Presumptuous, much? Maybe I'm a runner or a soccer player."

His gaze sweeps over me slowly and I hold my breath. "Are you?"

"N-no."

He laughs and takes a step away. "Noon. That's what time I eat lunch, in case you want to get here early or join me."

He gives me his back before I come up with a witty response. I can't decide if that was flirty banter or him really asking me to have lunch with him, but I figure it's best not to dissect it too much and not to show up at noon. I might be ready to sing all the single girl anthem songs, but I am not ready to start planning my schedule around cute boys. No matter how very, *very* cute they are. The only thing I've made any sense of from my breakup with Bryan is that I need to figure out who I am and what I want, make my own friends. Over the two years Bryan and I dated I grew farther and farther apart from my other friends. To the point, I really don't have any good girlfriends to call up and cry on their shoulder.

This is my fresh start.

I find English Composition easy enough. It's a big class in a room with long rows of seats, many of which are already taken.

I take a spot in the middle trying not to appear too eager or too much like a slacker. I don't mind English, but I'm not a fan of being called on in class either.

After English I have algebra and I'm not quite as confident about where the building for it is located. The Valley campus is pretty big, and the number of people walking around makes it hard to get my bearings. I slip my thumbs around the straps of my backpack and fall into the crowd of students, hoping I look like I fit in and don't have FRESHMAN stamped on my forehead.

I'm backtracking to find Moreno Hall when my front pocket vibrates. I pull out my phone and move off the sidewalk onto the grass, so I don't get trampled.

Adam: Get lost yet?

I glance up at the building that is most definitely not Moreno Hall.

Me: Of course not, but say I was looking for Moreno Hall...
Adam: Hang a left just past the engineering building, it's on the corner—big fancy-ass looking building, can't miss it.

A minute later he follows up.

Adam: Find it?
Me: I would have found it on my own eventually.
Adam: I'm sure.

Hurriedly, I pocket my phone and head to Moreno Hall.

By the end of the day, I'm exhausted but even more excited about the semester. All of my classes seemed okay, I met a few girls on our hall, and Ava and I spent the late afternoon walking around campus and soaking in all the first-day excitement.

I don't even think about Bryan until we get back to the dorm and I'm lying on my bed listening to Ava and Trent share first-day stories. I consider texting him for all of a millisecond. I don't hate him. Maybe I should. It'd probably be easier to get over him that way, but despite the awful way he ended things, I don't totally blame him for taking a great opportunity. And I'm working on not blaming him for not even wanting to try to make it work. Of course, I don't text him. Mostly because I don't think I can handle hearing how awesome everything is on his end. Not when the most notable part of my day was watching a table of jocks devour food like they hadn't eaten in months.

Over the next few days, I don't have any more hockey team run-ins. Which might be in part because Ava and I stock up on noodles and have lunch in our room most days and when I do go to the dining hall, I avoid the back table. My brother's teammates all seemed nice, but I'm not interested in continually being referred to as Adam Scott's baby sister.

Adam texts me every day to check in and invites me over to his place to hang out. I finally give in and agree to dinner Thursday night.

"Are you going to the dorm social tonight?" Ava asks that afternoon as we're hanging out in the room. I'm watching a new makeup tutorial, and she's letting me practice on her. I know a lot of people like to use themselves as a model, but I've never been one for wearing much makeup. Putting it on other people, though, makes me insanely happy.

"Can't. I'm having dinner with my brother. Tomorrow night? I've heard several fraternities are having parties."

"Trent is coming to town this weekend. I meant to ask how you felt about him staying in the dorm? If it makes you uncomfortable, we'll get a hotel."

"He's coming to visit already?"

She grins wide and the raspberry red color I've put on her lips looks fantastic. "Yeah, we've worked it out so we can visit each other almost every weekend this semester."

I hadn't given much thought to what we'd do when he was visiting. I grab a gloss and she parts her lips to let me coat them with a little shine. "He should stay here, of course."

"Cool. Thank you. Trent was stressing about coming up with the money for a hotel. The only one in town that's reasonably priced looks like it also rents by the hour." She pulls her mouth down into a grimace. "But it'll be fun. You'll like him."

"I'm excited to meet him. What are you guys going to do?"

"I'm not sure. Maybe the football game, maybe skipping it to make out." She blushes.

I nod, suddenly imagining a weekend of trying to ignore the sex sounds coming from the other side of the room.

Adam picks me up after he's done with classes for the day. I smile when his familiar Jeep comes into view. He stops at the curb outside of my dorm and I hop in.

"How's the first week?" he asks as he drives toward his apartment.

"Good. I think I'm finally getting a feel for the campus. It's sort of confusing—all the old buildings look the same. And what's up with the floor numbering in Emerson?"

He chuckles lightly. "How long did it take you to figure out there are two second floors?"

"Long enough that I was late to class."

"You'll have it memorized in no time and then you'll be laughing at the newbies getting lost."

"You're laughing at us?"

"Of course, we are." He winks.

"I think I might need to find a group or join something." I didn't do a lot of extracurricular activities in high school. I hung out with friends, I attended sporting activities and was always happy to cheer on my school, but there wasn't anything I cared about enough to dedicate my hours before or after school.

"Why's that?" Adam asks as he pulls into the parking lot of the apartment complex.

"Everyone here seems to be into something except me. The girls on my hall are great and I've met a few people in class, but they've all got a clique of people interested in the same things. The girls rushing sororities, the jocks, the nerds... I swear it's worse than high school."

He nods. "I guess that's true. I never thought about it before."

"That's because you came to college already in one of those cliques and with an instant group of friends."

"What about your roommate?"

"Ava's great, but she has a boyfriend at another college. I get the feeling she'll be spending a lot of her weekends visiting him or him visiting us." I scrunch up my nose. "He's staying with us this weekend."

"Did you find somewhere else to crash?"

"No. Why? It's my room too."

"Ginny, trust me, you need to find someone on your floor who'll let you stay in their room this weekend. Your dorm room is tiny, and they're going to be naked and going at it—that sounds hella uncomfortable for everyone. Unless you're into that sort of thing." Now he scrunches up his face. "Don't tell me if you are. I'd like to continue to believe my baby sister is asexual."

I snort laugh, but then everything he's saying hits me. "You're right. I can't stay there."

He nods. "There's always someone leaving on the weekends. Ask around and see who's heading out of town and will let you crash in their room."

"This is a thing. Seriously?"

"I lived in a suite, so it wasn't that big of a deal. I'd just crash on the couch in the living room."

"Ugh. I should have been a jock. Then I would have a ready-made clique and I wouldn't be getting kicked out of my own room."

"You're welcome to stay at my place."

"I'll figure it out." I appreciate him, but there has to be another option.

Adam's apartment isn't far from campus and if the number of vehicles with Valley University bumper stickers and license plate holders is indicative of how many students live here, then I'd say it's a lot.

He leads me up the stairs to the second-floor unit.

"Where is everyone?" I ask as we walk into the quiet living room.

"Campus or the gym." He drops his backpack on the couch. "We have preseason workouts twice a day this week. I'm gonna change real quick." He heads into one of the bedrooms off the living room.

"Where do you want to eat?" he calls through the open door.

"I don't care. Wherever you want."

I walk around the apartment scoping out my brother's living arrangements. There are three bedrooms, Adam's and then two on the opposite side of the unit. In the middle is an open concept area that has a kitchen, dining, and living room.

The place isn't that big but it's a pretty nice setup and feels huge by comparison to my tiny dorm room.

In the living room there's a matching couch and chair in a light brown leather. A coffee table, its top made of old hockey sticks, sits in front of the couch. The only artwork on the walls are a few jerseys and a hockey poster of the Bruins—Adam's favorite team.

The entire apartment is cleaner than I would have expected. A few empty Gatorade bottles on the kitchen counter, a football and a hockey stick—which I can't help but note is a random combination of sporting goods—lying in the middle of the floor in the living room, and a couple of stray articles of clothing on the backs of the chairs at the dining room table.

Adam reappears as I'm looking inside their empty refrigerator.

"Where's all your food?"

"We haven't gone shopping yet."

"What do you eat?"

He fills a glass with tap water and chugs it before responding. "We mostly eat on campus or we go out. We have a small kitchen in the locker room too that is re-stocked every few days."

"Can I use your bathroom before we go?" I head toward the one that is near his bedroom.

"Use the other one." He points to the bathroom on the opposite side of the apartment. "The light is out in mine. I need to get new bulbs."

"How do you see to shower or pee?" I ask.

"I leave the door open."

Boys are weird.

INSTEAD OF GOING TO A RESTAURANT, Adam and I go through a drive through and eat in his Jeep while he takes me all around Valley showing me Frat Row and some of the popular college bars and restaurants.

"Have you heard from Mom and Dad?" he asks. "Are they back from their trip?"

"They get back tomorrow, I think." Our parents went on some fancy, romantic vacation to Mexico. Initially I'd been bummed that they weren't going to be able to drop me off at college, but I'm glad they missed seeing me all sad and teary. The day Adam and I arrived on campus, I dropped my things in my room and then fell onto my new bed and sobbed. Poor Ava must have thought I was nuts.

"I'm really glad you're here," I admit.

He grins. "Me too. I get to spend the last year of college with my baby sister."

"You have to stop calling me that. I'm not a baby."

His mouth pulls into a wider smile. "Come over this weekend and crash at my place. You'll avoid listening to your roomie's sex sounds, and I'll introduce you to everyone. People are always coming and going from our apartment. It'll be good to meet more people here. Hell, maybe I'll throw a party."

"You never let me come to your parties in high school and now you're practically begging me. I find this quite redeeming even though now I don't actually want to go. Back then I would have killed to hang with you and your friends."

"High school was different. No one here cares if you're a freshman or senior or if you go to college at all. Plus, I want to see that you're settled. I know the shit with Bryan was rough."

I groan and Adam laughs.

"Only one condition. Promise me that you won't get wasted and make an ass of yourself in front of my teammates. I'm captain this year, and I need them to respect me."

"I promise," I say as I roll my eyes and toss a fry in his direction.

3

HEATH

"Carry me. My legs are dunzo." Maverick leans his sweaty, heavy frame against me.

"Get the fuck off. I'm barely standing on my own." I wobble and take a seat in my stall.

The first week of hell training is done and we survived... mostly. Coach Meyers likes to start out the year with a shit ton of conditioning and weight training. We won't even be allowed to step on the ice for another two weeks.

My buddy falls into the seat next to me and pulls a T-shirt over his head. "Wanna grab a drink at Prickly Pear?"

"I can't. Scott's called a house meeting," I say, annoyed and loud enough so Adam can hear me.

"Four-thirty. Don't be late," Adam says sternly. The rest of the guys are scared of him, being our team captain and all, but I know better. He's all talk. I push his buttons on a regular basis and I'm still standing despite him having a good three inches and fifteen pounds on me.

Maverick and I stop for alcohol to restock for the weekend. When we get back to the apartment, we settle into the couch for our house meeting.

I've only lived here for a month and this is the second meeting

Adam has called. It looks to be a long year. At least I have Mav for entertainment. He lives downstairs in a single apartment, but he spends way more time here than his own place.

His French bulldog, Charli, lies at his feet, staring up at him with adoring eyes. Charli is pretty much the only one who looks at Maverick like that. He's a total jokester and softie, but his size and tattoos intimidate most people.

Adam and Rauthruss wander out of their respective rooms. Rauthruss grabs a wooden chair from the dining table and Adam takes a seat in our leather recliner. He eyes the bottle in Maverick's hand. "Dude, really?"

"Ah, ah, ah," Mav tsks. "You can't speak until you have the bottle. New house rule." He hands it to Adam with a smirk. "Take a shot, captain, my captain."

"You don't even live here." Adam takes a long swallow of the MD 20/20 anyway and grimaces. "That shit's nasty. I haven't had Mad Dog since high school."

"Ironically, that's the last time I got called to a family meeting, too," Mav points out, taking the bottle back.

"Yeah, well feel free to leave since, again, you don't live here, but this won't take long. Three things." He holds up his fingers like he's talking to children. I glance over at Mav as he runs a hand along his tattooed chest where he's spilled on himself and a trail of alcohol trickles down to his shorts. Okay, maybe we're more like overgrown toddlers than functioning men. Maverick and I like to have fun, so sue us. We show up on the ice where it matters.

"Number one," Adam goes right into it. "We looked like shit out there this week."

Mav holds up a finger, takes a drink, and then speaks. "We're not even on the ice yet. Give it time."

Adam starts to respond, but not before Mav hands him the bottle and he begrudgingly takes another sip. "No, it's my last year and I'm not taking any chances by waiting for ice time. I think we should invite the guys over."

"Party. Good call," I say and find the bottle thrust into my side.

As I'm taking a drink, Adam shakes his head. "No, not a party. Well, okay, a party, but no girls. Just the team."

"You want us to spend our nights with a bunch of sweaty guys now too?" We're already spending long days in conditioning together. The only thing that got me through the week was the promise of a weekend of fun. "I'm not sure more time together is the answer."

"Girls," Mav says. "The answer is always girls. Let's get the freshmen laid."

"That's actually not a bad plan," Rauthruss speaks up for the first time. The bottle is passed to him and he fingers the label as he finishes. "Maybe they just need to let off a little steam."

Adam frowns and the vein in his forehead becomes noticeable —never a good sign. "We party all the time. The guys don't need our help finding chicks. This is about coming together as a team."

"You're going to go all weekend without your latest girlfriend?" Mav asks Adam pointedly.

Adam always has a girlfriend. I can't remember the current one's name. Hannah? Holly? I don't understand why he doesn't stay single. It isn't like he, or any of us for that matter, need the relationship label to get laid. But, no, Adam Scott is the full boyfriend experience. He doesn't only hook up or go on a few dates. He wastes months on these girls, going all in with dates and sleepovers... just not for more than six months or so at a time. He's an odd duck.

Rauthruss too. He's been dating the same girl since high school and she lives in freaking Nebraska. Why have a girlfriend you never see? The only perk of having a girlfriend is getting laid on a regular basis, right? I'm really asking; I have no idea.

"Maria and I broke up," he says with a shrug. "And it's just for tonight."

Maria. Wow, definitely off there.

"What happened to Heather?" Mav asks.

Ah, yes, Heather! My memory isn't failing me yet.

"They broke up in May. Keep up." Rauthruss reaches out for the

Mad Dog again, but Maverick holds it up and shakes the empty bottle. Fuck, we went through that fast.

"Fine. Party tonight. No girls," Mav says and looks to me. I'm the last holdout. "It's one night, man."

"What are the other two things on the agenda. We'll circle back," I say with a smile and Mav chuckles.

"Nice. Circling back. I think my dad used that the last time we talked."

His dad is a big executive—suit and tie, phone permanently attached to his ear. Rich as sin, but kind of a prick, so we have a bit of fun at his expense with our corporate speak, or jargon, if you will.

Adam interrupts our joking, which to be fair is probably the only way to get us back on track. "Number two. Heath, you have to walk your dates out the door. Like personally see that they make it outside." He looks to Rhett who's turning a nice shade of red.

Mav gasps dramatically with a hand to his chest. Charli at his feet lifts her head to check on her owner. "Heath would never. He's a true gentleman."

"It was one time and I did walk her out." I glance at my flushed roommate. The memory of him all bed head and in his boxers kicking out a half-naked Kimberly still makes me smile. "I just didn't lock the door behind her. How was I supposed to know she was going to come back and try to work her way around the apartment?"

I mean, seriously... is it my fault that she broke into our place and slipped into bed with the guy? Apparently nothing is sexier or more challenging for a girl than a guy in a real committed relationship. And Rauthruss is as loyal as they come even though he barely sees his woman. It drives girls crazy. Seriously, he could have any chick he wanted. He might be onto something, not that I have any plans to try his method. Mine's working just fine.

Maverick sets the empty bottle on the coffee table and heaves a sigh. "Are there any items on your list that don't revolve around our dicks?"

No one speaks. Adam raises his brows and keeps his sharp stare on me.

"Agreed. I will walk them out." I'm almost positive I can remember to do that. Definitely can tonight since I'll be spending it with my hand apparently.

"Next item on the agenda," Mav prompts.

Adam looks a little nervous, pausing before he speaks. This can't be good.

"My sister is crashing here this weekend, so best behavior." He stands.

"What the hell? What happened to no chicks?" I ask.

"She's my sister, not the same thing."

"Depends. Is she hot?" Mav asks, totally serious, which makes the vein in Adam's head protrude.

Yes, yes she is. I keep that to myself. I'm not scared of Scott, but I'm not an idiot. If he knew my unfiltered thoughts on his little sister, I'd be neutered in my sleep. Nah, actually, he'd probably do it when I was wide awake. Can't really blame him. Ginny Scott is sexy as hell and all my thoughts about her are dirty.

Long, blonde hair, light brown eyes, and her legs... those long legs are the things dreams are made of.

"Best behavior." Adam pulls his phone out and walks toward his room.

"Meeting adjourned then, eh?" Mav says and then looks to me. "I'm gonna need a copy of the minutes on my desk by end of business."

"I'm right on top of that, sir," I say and give him the middle finger.

"What the hell are we going to do tonight?" Mav looks seriously defeated as he runs a hand through his dark hair.

"Halo?" Rauthruss lifts an Xbox controller.

"Why the fuck not." He pets Charli and grabs the controller with the other hand.

I get up and take a step toward my room. "I'm going to shower and touch base with myself."

Mav cackles. "Not as good as circling back, but good wordplay. Mariah or Ariana for inspiration music?"

"It's definitely a Mariah kind of day," I decide.

Mav hums as I walk by. "'Santa Baby' or 'Heartbreaker'?"

I shake my head. "'Fantasy.' Always 'Fantasy.'"

LATER, I close my door so I can hear Nathan on the phone over the noise in the living room. A few guys have already made it over. I hope Scott's right, and this is what we need. He might be a pain in the ass, but he's not wrong about us needing to play better together. It's his last year, so I get the extra pressure to make it the best before he's done.

He's not interested in playing professionally, so this really is it for him.

"How does it feel to be back?"

"Not as good as it would feel to be practicing with the Coyotes right now," I say as I take a seat at my desk.

He snickers. "Soon enough."

"Eh," I grunt. I've never been much for living in the future. Even now that it's set. I signed with Arizona's professional team over the summer. Three more years at Valley and then I'll get paid to play hockey. It still hasn't really sunk in. "How's everything in Florida?"

"Good. Busy. Between the team and all the wedding plans, it's gotten nuts. Did you get the save the date?"

"I did." I pick up the thick paper invitation on my desk. "June, huh? You really think you can continue to not screw this up for another ten months?"

"God, I hope so. I don't know what I'll do if she wises up before then," he says in a teasing voice. I can hear his fiancée Chloe in the background taunting him back but can't make out her words.

"Tell her I said hey and thanks for the giant box of stuff. This one's got Chloe written all over it. A gift card to The Olive Garden?"

Nathan speaks away from the phone, "Busted. Totally called you out on The Olive Garden gift card."

"Take a nice girl to dinner," Chloe yells.

"You hear that?" my brother asks.

"Yeah, I got it."

They've been sending me packages every month since my freshman year. Each one is different and contains shit ranging from razors, body wash, homemade oatmeal raisin cookies (my favorite), to new clothes and cologne. And then there's the gift cards. Each month, a hundred dollars or more from random places.

Since I refuse to take money outright from Nathan, they find creative ways to be generous. I don't really need it. I have a full-ride scholarship for hockey and a part-time job that helps with anything else. But that's Nathan, always trying to take care of me.

"All right, well I won't keep you. Chloe and I are headed to the beach. Stay out of trouble."

I groan and tilt my head back.

With a chuckle, Nathan says, "I'm proud of you, but what kind of big bro would I be if I didn't remind you not to screw up? You've got more than ever on the line."

"Oh, I don't know, the cool kind maybe?"

"Have fun. I'll call you next week. Let me know if you need anything. Oh, and call Mom. She said she hasn't heard from you in two weeks."

"Been busy."

"Mhmm, weak excuse. Later, Heath."

"Bye, Heath," Chloe says in the background.

"Bye, guys, talk to you later."

4

GINNY

Trent arrives late Friday afternoon and Ava is brimming with excitement. She introduces me and then recaps a list of facts about the guy. Facts she's already told me several times. I feel like I know him better than I know Ava at this point; she's told me *that much* about him. Maybe a little too much.

"I'm going to show him around campus and then we're going to the football game. Do you want to come with us?" She's practically beaming with happiness and I have a twinge of sadness that this could be me and Bryan if he weren't in freaking Idaho.

She leans into his side and Trent wraps an arm around her waist. His fingers slip under the hem of her T-shirt and he kisses her forehead.

It's obvious how much they've missed one another by the touchy-feely display in front of me, and I'm starting to understand just how imperative it is I get the hell out of here. I haven't even been able to bring myself to watch porn since Bryan broke up with me. I certainly can't handle a full-on romantic display with a side of orgasms.

"No, thanks. You two enjoy. My brother is having people over, so I'm going to go hang with them. You two will have the place all to yourself tonight. It was really nice to meet you, Trent."

I shower and get ready, hesitant to head over to Adam's before the party gets going. I appreciate that he always looks out for me, but I want to find my own friends at Valley, too, and if I run over there every time I need an escape, I'm going to spend the next year as Adam Scott's little sister instead of Ginny Scott. So tonight, I need to find some friends.

I text Adam to make sure he's there before driving over.

Adam: Yep. Just hanging out at the house. You coming over? I warned the guys to be on their best behavior.
Me: Yes, but please don't make it weird. I know you and your friends are disgusting. You don't need to warn them like I'm some sort of delicate flower.

I ignore the rest of his messages that pop up, telling me he's only looking out for me or whatever. Having an older, overbearing brother is a real pain sometimes.

The apartment is easy enough to find and I carry my backpack with a change of clothes and toothbrush up to the second-floor door and knock.

"You must be Little Scott." A guy with a shit ton of tattoos on full display thanks to his bare chest greets me with a goofy smile. "I'm Johnny Maverick."

"Ginny."

He pulls the door wide and I enter. A bunch of guys I don't recognize are standing around the apartment. For real, it's like I just entered the men's locker room with the way they all stop what they're doing and stare at me.

Adam's head pops up from the kitchen and he hustles forward. "Did you find it okay?"

"Yeah. I have this thing called maps on my phone."

I spot Rhett in the living room and he lifts a controller in greeting. "Hey, Ginny. Good to see you again."

I wave awkwardly. They're all still staring.

Adam shuts the door and I follow him into the living room. He points to the guy who answered the door. "You met Maverick. Ignore any and everything he says."

He scoffs. "I am hilarious and awesome."

"That's Liam, Jordan, and Tiny."

"Hey," they say in unison.

"Want something to eat or drink?" my brother asks and goes back to the kitchen.

"I'm okay for now." There's an empty seat next to Maverick, so I head for it and sit down.

"Where is Payne?" one of the guys asks him.

"Still showering and jerking it to Mariah, probably." Maverick stills, looks to me, and clears his throat. "Shit, sorry."

I laugh and wave him off. "Good for him. And Mariah."

"I like you." Maverick puts his arm around me on the back of the couch, but it's in a friendly way that doesn't feel like he's hitting on me.

"Hands off," Adam's deep voice bellows from the kitchen.

Maverick rolls his eyes and I'm glad he's not so easily intimidated by my brother. It was a real issue in high school before Adam graduated. He would look at guys the wrong way for talking to me and they'd scamper off too afraid of him.

He stands and looks down at me. "You need a drink? A smoke?"

"Yeah, I think I might need a drink after all."

The party, or what's arrived of it, moves outside on the deck off the kitchen of the apartment. It's nice out. Still hot like August nights always are in Arizona, but a nice breeze and the cold drink in my hand helps. Even Adam seems to relax as the guys kick back with their beers. It's still just the guys on the team, but it's early.

"I'm going to get another drink." I head inside to the bathroom and have to use the flashlight on my phone to see anything. Why my brother hasn't changed the light bulb is beyond me.

I can't really see much in the mirror, enough to make out my French braid is mostly still intact. In the kitchen, I rummage through the refrigerator looking for something besides beer, but it's that or Wild Turkey. Definitely no.

As I turn, movement catches my eye and I jump in surprise. "You scared me."

He grins, hand gliding through the wet hair sticking up on his head like he ran a towel through it and said fuck it. He looks me over carefully. I'm frozen, my tongue feels heavy or too wide for my mouth or something.

"Hey, Ginny."

"Hi." I look around dumbfounded. I'd expected to run into him, but not half-naked. "Do you live here?"

"Well, I don't usually walk around in my boxers at other dude's houses." He looks to the ceiling and a smirk pulls at his lips. "Well, not often."

I'd been actively avoiding the wall of nakedness in front of me, but now that he's acknowledged it, I can't look away.

The only thing he wears are a pair of gray boxer briefs that hug his huge thighs and—oh my god, Ginny, do not look at his crotch. Shit, too late. I tear my gaze away from the bulge and up to his abs. Forget a boring six-pack, Heath has ridges and lines that wrap around his midsection. I follow the line to his chest and biceps. It shouldn't be possible for someone to look this good naked.

And oh my God, stop looking already!

Adam comes through the door before I can make words come out of my mouth.

"Payne, fucking finally. We thought you drowned in there." Adam tosses his empty in the trash and grabs another beer, his face hardening as he gets a good look at him. "Dude, what the hell? Put some clothes on in front of my sister."

"Relax, I didn't know she was here yet." Heath's tone is agitated, rightfully so.

"Pants, dude. Now."

"Adam," I admonish.

"And no hitting on my baby sister." His demeanor relaxes slightly, and he punches Heath playfully in the arm, although it seems a little harder than necessary.

"Are you coming back outside?" Adam asks me, pausing at the door that leads to the deck.

"I'll be right there," I assure him.

Heath brushes by me, the heat of his body licking flames up my arm and grabs two beers from the fridge. He hands one to me. "So, I hear you're sleeping with me this weekend."

"Umm... what?"

"I hear you're sleeping at our place this weekend." He leans a hip against the counter and pops the top off the beer.

"Right. Yeah. My roommate's boyfriend is in town for the weekend."

"Lucky for us."

"I doubt you guys will even know I'm here."

"One chick among twenty-seven guys? Plus, it's you. You're kind of hard to miss." His eyes drop to my mouth.

"One chick? Please. Actually, I'm surprised there aren't girls over already. Are you hiding an orgy in your room?"

He laughs. It's a deep, playful tone that lights up my insides. "I wish." He pushes off the counter. "Your brother has banned girls from the apartment tonight."

"What? Why?" That doesn't sound like Adam.

"Team building or some shit. Just you and the team, Ginny Scott."

"No. Absolutely not. Adam said he was going to introduce me to people, not hang with his bros."

With a light chuckle, he lifts his beer and takes a drink making me realize I haven't touched mine.

"I'm going to kill him."

"Well, that I want to see. I better get dressed." He winks and heads down the hall on the opposite side of the apartment from Adam's room. I'm finally able to take a breath again. Holy mother of all that is good, he's a lot.

I head outside and take a seat next to Adam. "No girls? What the hell? I thought you wanted to introduce me to people."

He looks conflicted on how to respond. "I will. I am." He motions around the party.

"People besides your teammates, Adam." I flail my hands around. "Girls."

"Yeah, let's get some girls over here," someone says and Adam scowls at them over my head and then drops his gaze back to me.

"Please?" I ask quieter. "I'm sure your teammates are great, but I don't want to hang with a bunch of dudes all weekend."

"Shit, Ginny, I didn't even think about Bryan and what it might be like to be around a bunch of guys..." He rubs at the back of his neck. "All right, yeah, let's have a real party."

That wasn't exactly what I'd meant by not wanting to hang out with a bunch of dudes, but if it gets girls over here, I will keep my mouth shut and let him think it's my sad, I hate all of mankind broken heart speaking.

"On it," Maverick says and pulls out his phone.

5

HEATH

A knock brings my attention to the door and Scott's head peeks in. "Hey, I'm going to run to the store to get more alcohol. You need anything?"

"Are you sure I'm allowed out of my room?" I ask. I still haven't bothered to get dressed. I sat down at my desk to check in with work and got distracted.

"Sorry, man, I'm a little protective of her. She's been through a lot."

I nod and open my top desk drawer and pull out the stack of gift cards. "Where are you going?"

"Dude, what all you got there?" He laughs and walks closer.

"Gift cards to pretty much every place you can think of."

His eyes widen. "You're coming with me. Bring your stash."

I don't know what his sister said to him, but in an hour's time, our place has become packed with guys *and girls*. *Good work, Ginny.*

Adam and I head out and make several stops getting booze and food. When we're on our way back, I finally decide to broach the subject on my mind.

"Soooo... your sister's smoking hot."

I'm messing with him, sort of. She is smoking hot, but I'm only sharing this information to get a rise out of him. As predicted, he pins me with a hard stare. I meet it and smile, letting him know I'm not intimidated.

"Off-limits, Payne."

"Relax, I'm giving you shit. I don't do the whole girlfriend thing like you. We've only talked a few times. She's nice."

"She is. I worry about her. She doesn't know a lot of people at Valley yet and I want to introduce her to everyone, but she's off-limits. Friend zone only, man. I know how you are."

Ouch. I'm a perfect gentleman, thank you very much. Just because I don't date the same girl for months at a time, doesn't mean I treat them any worse.

"Is there some sort of big brother gene that makes you all giant overprotective assholes?"

"I'm serious. She just got out of a relationship and she doesn't need another guy screwing her over."

We pull up to the apartment and grab the bags to carry inside. Before we enter the apartment, Adam stops and regards me seriously. "You'll help me keep an eye on her? Make sure the rest of the guys don't mess with her?"

"She doesn't need a babysitter, man, and I'm no nanny."

His mouth pulls into a thin line and I cave, some part of me understanding his concern. I can't imagine having a little sister around my teammates and friends.

"I will keep an eye out, but I'm not going to lord over her like some sort of protector. Normal, friendly, keep an eye out, not whatever you've got going on there." I lift one of my arms bringing the grocery bags with it and motion to him and his moody intensity.

"Good enough, I guess."

I barely get the beer to the fridge before people are grabbing for it. I take two and spot the object of my and Adam's conversation sitting on the couch watching Maverick and Rauthruss play Halo.

"Hey," I say as I take a seat next to her and hold out a beer. Her hair is in an elaborate looking braid, the end hanging over one shoulder.

She takes the can hesitantly. "Thanks."

"Where's mine?" Maverick teases.

"In the fridge."

He holds a hand to his chest and pretends to be appalled.

"When you're as hot as Ginny, I'll start being your beer bitch, too."

She rolls her eyes as she pops the tab on her beer, but there's a faint blush to her cheeks.

"Genevieve," Adam calls from the kitchen and lifts a beer in a silent offering. She holds up the one I gave her so he can see she's already got one.

"Genevieve?" Mav asks. "I thought your name was Ginny."

"Ginny is short for Genevieve."

"That's rad. Why would you ever go by anything else?" He says her name again slowly. "Genevieve."

"Adam couldn't pronounce it when I was born."

Mav and Rauthruss bust up laughing.

"He was three," she adds, sticking up for him.

Rauthruss wins, like he always does, and Mav looks to me. "I'm done getting my ass kicked. Do you want to play?"

Nodding, I hold a hand up and he tosses the controller to me. I nudge Ginny. "What do you say?"

Rauthruss holds his out to her and she takes it.

"Have you played before?"

"I grew up with Adam. What do you think?" She sits forward and places her beer on the coffee table and straightens her shoulders. She's taking this seriously, looking determined and sexy as hell.

I set out with the goal of taking it easy on her, but Ginny doesn't need it. A few of the guys on the team crowd around to cheer her on and voice their hope of me getting my ass kicked. I win, just barely, and everyone boos.

"Thanks a lot, guys. Real team spirit."

"Do over," she demands.

I'm not confident I can pull off a victory twice, so I hesitate. We lean forward and grab our beers at the same time. I take a long drink while she sips and then grimaces.

"What was that face?" I stare at her cute little mouth and pink lips wet from the beer.

"Do you actually like the taste of beer?" she asks.

"I wouldn't drink it otherwise. Why didn't you say something?"

"I'm trying to learn to like it. It seems to be what everyone drinks here." She takes a longer drink as if to prove her point.

"Be right back."

I find Jordan and trade a twenty-dollar gift card for a twelve-pack of his hard seltzers. Two more people have taken over the game, so I motion for Ginny to follow me and lead her out to the deck.

"Try this."

"Thank you." She takes it and I lean back against the railing. There are a lot of people out here, but no one is paying us any attention except her brother. Big brother radar, I guess. Dude needs to chill.

I turn so his big-headed scowl isn't in my peripheral. There's no pleasing the guy. He wanted me to look out for her. I am, yet he still seems displeased. "I don't remember seeing you last year. You were really at our games?"

"A few of them." This time when she takes a drink, she smiles. "Much better." She plays with the end of her braid. "I was at the Colorado game and Arizona State and whoever you guys played for Parent's Night."

I think back to that game for a second. "Western Michigan."

"Right." Her smile lifts higher.

"I can't believe I didn't see you." Her phone is stuck in the front pocket of her jeans and I nod toward it. "Let me see your phone."

She hands it over without question and I program my number in it and send myself a text so I have hers.

"A lot of people come to the games. Plus, it wasn't like I was sitting on the bench with the team. Do you guys notice anyone in the crowd?"

"We notice hot girls." Maverick butts into the conversation and puts an arm around her shoulders. "You're hot, Little Scott."

She blushes and I hand her phone back.

Mav holds on to her and takes a step away from me. "I'm stealing her. Ginny here has a lot of people dying to meet her and you're hogging her, Payne."

"I do?" Ginny asks, sounding a little hopeful.

"Oh yeah." Mav nods. "Come on. You need a tour guide."

"Okay, yeah, that'd be great." She glances at me. "You probably want to hang out with your friends anyway." She lifts her seltzer. "Thanks for this."

"Anytime, Genevieve." I wink and tug the end of her braid.

She follows Mav, and I head inside, grab another beer, and take a seat back on the couch next to Rauthruss's giant frame. "I've got winner."

6

GINNY

TRUE TO HIS WORD, Maverick introduces me to everyone. He has a shirt on now, but the tattoos that cover both arms, all the way down to his fingers, are still visible. And I can spot a hint of his chest ink peeking out of the top of his T-shirt.

He leads me to where Liam and Jordan are standing. Liam and Maverick look like polar opposites. Where Johnny Maverick is dark-haired and covered in tattoos, Liam is blond and clean cut. He's even wearing a polo shirt. Even though I met him earlier, this time when Maverick introduces me, Liam extends a hand for me to shake. "Ginny, really nice to meet you."

"Same." His politeness catches me by surprise, but I slip my hand into his giant palm and squeeze.

"Roadrunner?" Jordan asks, holding a blue shot glass out to me.

I take it and sniff. "What's a Roadrunner?"

"It's like a Blue Kamikaze," he says and continues passing out shots.

I don't bother asking what a Blue Kamikaze is. My experience with alcohol is pretty limited. My high school bestie always grabbed a bottle of white wine from her parents' wine refrigerator and we'd drink that when we went to parties or had sleepovers. I never paid much attention to the label—none of it was great, but it was better than beer.

Jordan lifts his and the rest of us mimic the movement. I watch the others drink first. No one grimaces, so I take a sip. It's good, sweet. I smile and then drain the rest of the glass.

"We're off to meet more people," Mav tells them, pulling me away. He stops every couple of steps to make introductions and share the bottle of Mad Dog he's carrying. He's funny and kind of ridiculous, saying whatever pops into his head. Or maybe not, but if he's holding back at all—I don't want to think about the thoughts left unsaid.

"Total douche," he says after we're done talking to one guy that I think he said was a neighbor.

I laugh. "Then why did you introduce me to him?"

"Gotta know which ones to stay away from."

The next time he stops, it's in front of a girl standing by herself, her face hidden behind her phone. "Dakota, baby, I missed you all summer."

"You missed having someone to bum laundry detergent and junk food from." She looks up and over the device at Maverick. She's pretty. Big, ice-blue eyes and strawberry blonde hair that hangs in loose waves around her shoulders. She looks sweet, but the playful glare she gives Maverick makes me believe she could cut a bitch with words alone. That gaze slides to me and softens. "Hey."

"Dakota lives in the apartment next door. I'm her favorite neighbor." He tips his head to me. "This is Scott's little sister, Ginny."

"Hey there." I wave three fingers around my drink.

"Where's Reagan?" Maverick asks. Then to me, "Her roommate. The nicer of the two."

Dakota flips him off. "She'll be here. She was still getting ready. Ginny, you're a freshman?"

"Did the seltzer give it away?"

She lifts her cup. "We've got a better variety at our place if you want something else. These guys only know cheap beer and hard liquor."

"Thank you. That's really nice."

"Of course."

Dakota's phone pings, and she smiles at the screen. "Wardrobe emergency. I should go make sure Reagan's not buried under a pile of dresses. Do you want to come with me and scan our booze?"

Maverick nods his approval and smiles like a proud parent who's set up their kid on a successful playdate. "You two have fun. Don't tell her any lies about us, Dakota."

"Lies would be less incriminating."

Dakota lets us into her apartment across the breezeway from the guys.

"Help!" a muffled voice calls from one of the bedrooms. A girl with hair the color of honey pulled up in curlers rushes out wearing a silky robe. "I don't know what to wear."

Dakota laughs. "This is Ginny. Ginny, that's my neurotic but lovable roommate, Reagan."

"Hey," she says, breathless, cheeks pink.

"Green's a good color on you," I tell her and motion to the emerald color of her robe.

"She's right. Put on that green dress with the crisscross back."

Reagan smiles, deep dimples popping out. "Oh, right. I forgot about that one." She disappears back into the room.

Dakota moves to the kitchen and I hang in the living room looking around.

"I like your apartment." It's decorated with lots of black and white with pops of dark pink. Old Hollywood movie posters and cute furniture. It's a smaller version of my brother's, but same basic setup with bedrooms on either side of the living area.

"Thanks," she says, and I join her in the kitchen area. "Pick your poison." A wide selection of alcohol is spread out on their kitchen counter. Wine—red and white, hard lemonade, vodka, Captain Morgan, and a bunch of mixers. I settle on half a cup of white wine. After all the mixing, I'm a little nervous to drink too much.

"So, you're Adam Scott's little sister?" she asks with a smirk once we both have a fresh drink.

"I am. Yeah. You know him?"

"Everyone knows him. He's Adam Scott."

Reagan reappears in green with her hair down, looking like she walked out of a salon. If I could make that sort of transformation in five minutes, I'd probably get dolled up more often.

"Do we have a winner?" Dakota asks.

Reagan holds her arms out to her sides. "I think so."

"You look great." I glance down at my jeans and tank top. I'm underdressed by comparison. Dakota's in a skirt and T-shirt with tennis shoes, but her makeup and jewelry give it all a much more put-together look than my casual outfit. "Do you guys always dress up like this for parties?"

Dakota responds first. "This is my basic uniform, but that one" —she nods toward her roommate— "has her eye on a boy."

Reagan makes a face at her but smiles.

"Oooooh. Someone at the party?" I ask. "One of the hockey guys?"

"Yeah." She takes a seat next to me.

"She won't say which one. I've got money on Liam. He's got that nice guy vibe, but something about him screams that he's probably not afraid to get down and dirty in the sheets." Dakota pours white wine into a cup and hands it to Reagan.

"Liam? Really?" Reagan asks with a shake of her head. "He's not my type. And I'm not saying who because I don't want to jinx it."

"Well, he'd be a fool to turn you down," I tell her honestly. Reagan is the kind of pretty that you wish only existed on the pages of a magazine or on TV.

She takes the drink and sighs. "I'm nervous, which is ridiculous, right? Who gets nervous about going to a party where their crush is? It's like junior high all over except without the zits and braces. Thank god. I've been trying to talk to this guy for... a long time. I get all weird and shy around him. Well, shier than normal."

"You're going to knock his socks off. Trust me." Dakota says. "And if not, you get to come home to me."

"Have you guys been roommates for a long time?" I ask. It's easy to see how close they are. They tease, but it's with a smile and none of the catty, fake compliments that some girls do to one another.

"Since our freshmen year in the dorms," Reagan answers. "Dakota was all fast-talking and no-nonsense, and I think I spent half of first semester completely terrified of her."

Dakota laughs. "It's true. She said maybe three full sentences until she saw me crying over *The Notebook*."

"She was *sobbing*."

"Those old people get me every time."

They smile at one another and then Reagan adds, "We moved out as soon as we could last year."

Even though Reagan and Dakota are two years older than me, we fall into an easy camaraderie. They tell me more about their time in the dorms together and they ask me about Ava and how my first week went.

When we finally fall silent, my cheeks hurt from smiling.

"I can see it," Dakota says looking me over closely. "You've got the same eyes and smile."

This makes Reagan look between us and when her brown eyes land on me, they narrow as she studies me. "Same eyes and smile as who?"

"Ginny is Adam's sister."

"Adam Scott?" she asks, eyes widening through thick, black lashes.

Man, it really pains me that even someone as beautiful as Reagan has this reaction about my brother. At least my high school friends hid their fascination with him better.

"That's the one." My phone buzzes in my front pocket and I pull it out. "That's him, checking in. He's a total pain in the ass." I type back a response letting him know I'm next door.

"Everyone ready?" Dakota asks.

Reagan and I nod.

Dakota leads the way. "Let's do this."

Hanging out with Dakota and Reagan is fun. They know everyone, and after the initial shock of finding out I was Adam's little sister, they haven't made me feel like the other Scott.

Speaking of the popular Scott, when I finally spot him, he's in the corner with his arm wrapped around a girl I haven't met. He leans down and whispers in her ear and she giggles and tips her mouth up to let him kiss her. Gross. Seeing my brother in action—really not cool.

"What do women see in him?" I huff. "I mean, honestly?" I turn to Reagan and Dakota.

"Dude, your brother's hot." Dakota shrugs. "Sorry."

I scrunch up my face and walk toward him. He comes up for air when I clear my throat.

"Ginny." He pulls the girl tighter to his side and then nods to Dakota and Reagan. "I see you two met my sister."

"Yeah, she's way cooler than you. What happened?" Dakota deadpans.

"Tough crowd." Adam tilts his head to the girl still clinging to him. "Guys, this is Taryn."

"Hey." Her red lips pull up into a big smile. "Your brother's told me so much about you."

"Oh really?" I ask, surprised since he's never mentioned her, but I smile because I'm not an asshole, and it isn't her problem my brother jumps from girl to girl. "Well, it's nice to meet you." I give Reagan and Dakota a *save me* look, which they interpret quickly and make excuses for us.

"How does he already have a new girlfriend?"

Neither of them answers, not that I expected them to.

"It's the hot thing," Dakota says. "And the hockey thing."

"We should hang out tomorrow," Reagan offers.

"Are you coming to the pool party?" Dakota asks.

"What pool party?"

"Oh yeah, you should definitely come." Reagan smiles. I freaking love her dimples. "It's at The White House. It's a big, back to school party they have every year. Everyone will be there."

"I'm in." And just like that, I'm pretty sure I've made two new friends here.

7

GINNY

Ginny

The next morning, I'm sitting outside on the deck FaceTiming with Reagan and Dakota recapping last night. I had so much fun and I'm excited to hang out with them again today.

Adam comes out, shirtless, hair matted from sleep, and a giant bottle of Gatorade in hand. "'Morning."

"Hey."

He takes a seat next to me with a big, tired sigh and glances to the phone in my hand with a smile. Which reminds me...

"Reagan, what happened with that guy last night?"

"Oh, nothing." She bites at the corner of her lip, making one dimple dot her cheek. "It was stupid. He's dating someone else. I didn't realize until last night. Moving on."

"How is that possible? You're gorgeous. Did you tell him you were into him?"

She shakes her head.

I angle the phone so she can see Adam. "Would you tell her that she needs to tell this guy so he can break up with his girlfriend to date her?"

He chuckles and Reagan's eyes go wide. "Oh my god, Ginny. Adam, you absolutely do not need to—"

"She's right." He nods and smiles at my new friend. "Guy must be crazy."

"See. Told you."

She covers her face with her hands like she's embarrassed.

"I'm going to hang with Adam for a bit."

"Hurry up and get over here," Dakota says, popping her head in front of the screen for a second.

"I'll be over soon," I promise.

"Looks like you made some friends," Adam says as I hang up the phone.

"I did. Thanks for letting me crash in your room last night."

"No problem. The couch wasn't too bad."

"That might have had something to do with the girl that was on it with you."

"Probably so," he agrees. "Do you girls want to ride over to the party together?"

"Sure, sounds good." I stand and stretch. "See you later."

I knock at Dakota and Reagan's and then open the door. "Hello?"

"In my room," Reagan calls.

Dakota sits on the bed and Reagan tosses two giant handfuls of swimsuits onto the comforter.

"I pulled all my suits for you to choose from," Reagan says.

I didn't bring a bathing suit from the dorm, so I'm thankful she's letting me borrow one but holy crap. "That is a lot of options."

She nods happily.

I shower and pull my hair into a braid. I go for a low-cut pink one-piece suit and my own cut-off shorts and sandals.

I'm waiting on Dakota and Reagan's couch while they finish getting ready when I get a text.

Hottest guy on campus: Did you leave without saying goodbye? <sad face>
Me: Who is this and how did you get this number?
Hottest guy on campus: Name is self-explanatory.

It is self-explanatory, sadly. I met dozens of people last night, but Heath is the only one I can recall with any detail. There's a hotness about Heath that goes beyond types and is more universal truth.

Hottest guy on campus: Back at the dorm?
Me: No, actually I'm next door waiting for Dakota and Reagan so we can leave for the pool party. Are you going?
Hottest guy on campus: Depends. Are you going to be there in a bikini?

I glance down at my very covered midsection.

Me: Guess you'll have to come to find out.

Despite Heath's texts that sound anxious to see me, he isn't around when Dakota, Reagan, and I meet Adam and Rhett in the parking lot to catch a ride over.

We pile into Adam's Jeep and drive the few blocks to the pool party. Adam parks along the street and points. "That's Ray Fieldhouse. The student fitness facility is inside, and a lot of the teams have private workout rooms there, too."

"Where's the rink from here?" I ask, trying to get my bearings. The Valley U campus is big and I'm still not sure where everything is.

"Couple of blocks west," Rhett answers.

I sling my beach bag over my shoulder and follow the guys up the sidewalk. "Whose house is this?" I ask once we get to our destination. I was expecting an apartment with a community pool or an old house with a tiny yard and pool. This is none of that.

"This is The White House," Adam remarks. "Guys from the basketball team live here."

We walk around to the back of the giant white house, aptly named, to the pool party going on outside. The pool itself takes up half the large yard and the other side is grassy with a volleyball net set up. There are people everywhere. *Everywhere.* The scene looks like something straight out of a spring break video. Music pumping loudly, girls lounging on rafts, guys chilling with beers in hand, a coed volleyball game.

Even in my tiny shorts and my cleavage pushed up to my ears, I'm grossly overdressed. And where does one stow a bag in a place like this? Something tells me I'm not going to need any of the things I packed: sunscreen, towels, bottled water, three pairs of sunglasses.

On the plus side, there are entirely too many people in the back yard of The White House to feel uncomfortable or self-conscious about my giant bag. My thoughts only stray as far as my next step.

We squeeze through behind Adam and Rhett's large frames to the keg. I'm introduced to more guys from the hockey team, some I recognize from last night.

"Tiny?" I can't help but ask of the guy who is anything but. "Your name is Tiny?"

Tiny, I find out once I have a beer in hand, is a nickname because Tony Waklsinski is the shortest player on the team. And I guess in comparison with Adam, who's at least five inches taller, I can sort of see it. I know how sensitive boys are about inches.

Maverick finds us and joins the circle. Today he's wearing a brightly colored Hawaiian shirt left open to reveal his chiseled abs and tattoos. He lifts the bottle of Mad Dog in his hand. "Shot?"

The other girls pass, but I'm feeling adventurous, so I take it and tip it back, letting some of the sweet liquid slide down my throat. I grimace; it's so sickly sweet that I chase it with beer, which doesn't really help since I'm not a fan of it either.

"All right. Let's not get my baby sister shitfaced." Adam takes the bottle and takes a drink three times as big as mine as if he's trying to drink it all so I won't.

"Anyone seen Payne? He's supposed to be bringing reinforcements." Maverick reaches for the nearly empty bottle and gives it a shake.

"No clue," Adam says. "Thought he was with you."

When Taryn shows up with her friends, that feels like my cue to leave.

"Mingle?" I ask Dakota and Reagan.

We make a circle around the party and head inside to check out the drink selection. "This is not what I thought of when you guys said pool party."

"It's more bikini party unless you're brave enough to get in the pool," Reagan says.

"What's wrong with the pool?"

"Going into the pool is the equivalent of posting an *I'm here to get laid* sign on your forehead," Dakota says. "Which if you're into that, it's totally fine, but don't say I didn't warn you." She holds up the vodka in invitation. "Drink?"

After we swap out our beer for vodka and tonic, we head back outside.

We sit on lounge chairs on the patio near a mister and watch the people in the pool. Some love matches (or rather, hookups) are being made while other people are being hilariously blown off.

Dakota drills me with twenty questions while we people watch. Now that we've spent a little time together, she holds nothing back, but somehow the way she pries is endearing.

"So, no boyfriend?" Reagan asks, leaning forward with her elbows on her knees.

"No," I say with a scowl.

Dakota laughs. "Oooh, there's a story."

"Not a good one."

Water drips onto my toes and I look up to see Maverick leaning over and shaking his head on us.

"Bad dog," Dakota scolds him.

I'm laughing as I dodge him continuing to get us wet when my gaze falls to a guy approaching from behind him.

"Ah, there he is," Maverick says, taking a seat next to me. "Payne, where the hell have you been?"

"Been around." His dark blue eyes land on me. He's got a twelve-pack of hard seltzer under one arm and my stomach flips.

He pulls a bottle of Mad Dog out of his pocket and hands it to Maverick.

"Trade you." He motions with his head and Maverick stands, giving up his seat and taking the bottle.

He smells like soap and sun and wild dreams. Dreams you shouldn't allow because they're so out of reach, but you can't help but want. Dreams you don't speak of, but that live in the darkest corner of your mind.

"Swim anyone?" Maverick asks.

I shake my head as does Reagan.

"Oh, why not." Dakota stands, looks to me and shrugs with a smirk

"I'm going to find the bathroom. Do you want to come?" Reagan asks me, then glances between me and Heath.

"I'm good."

Heath opens the case and holds out a can. "Drink?"

As I wrap my hands around the cold can, he holds tight and leans in. "You look good. Do you want to skip this party and go make out?"

I laugh, but heat rushes to my core at the thought. "Pass."

"You wanna not skip this party and just make out right here?"

"Definitely pass." I pull the drink from his hand and pop the top. After I've taken a long drink, I ask, "Does that usually work for you?"

"Honestly?"

I nod.

"Every time."

I roll my eyes. "What is wrong with women?"

"I'm really good at making out." His stare darts to my mouth. I have no doubt.

"You and I are going to be just friends."

"Friends?" His brows raise. "I don't have girl friends."

"You do now."

―――

THANKS FOR READING this sample of Secret Puck. All the books in the series can be read as a standalone, but here's the reading order.

Secret Puck
Bad Crush
Broken Hearts
Wild Love

TUTORING THE PLAYER

CAMPUS WALLFLOWERS BOOK ONE

I have a type.

I love the good guy.

Responsible and stable. Safe.

So when a beer-drinking, quick-witted, tattooed hockey player asks me to tutor him, I'm suddenly thrust into the world of bad boys and bad decisions.

Jordan is a renowned player on campus.

He doesn't take anything seriously, except hockey and partying.

But he gives me butterflies.

I'm a wallflower tutoring Valley University's hottest player.

PROLOGUE
DAISY

"Would you come down from there?" Violet yells up from the ground. My cousin isn't the biggest fan of heights or rickety ladders. "You're going to catch pneumonia or an airborne STD."

"They won the game," I say with a quick glance down at her.

She's standing on the lowest rung, neck craning up to see over the fence into our neighbor's yard. "Who cares? Win, lose, they party just the same."

She might talk like she's immune to the fun next door, but I've caught her wistfully staring out her bedroom window a time or two in that direction.

"They look so happy."

From my spot in this old tree house, I have a perfect view of the backyard next door. A small group of girls dance in the grass to a catchy, upbeat song. In another area, guys huddle together playing cornhole. Others are in the heated pool, splashing and playing. Everyone else is hanging out on the large patio that spans the back of the sprawling house.

The alcohol is flowing, and the atmosphere is so happy and light that the air even feels different this close.

"The night is young, and they're buzzed. Of course, they're

happy." Vi's tone is all indifference. "Give it a few hours, and people will be so drunk the happiness will dim."

She's wrong. At least once a week, I sit up here watching them drink and laugh, and I can attest that they leave as happy as they came.

"Come on," she whines. "You promised we'd finish *Pride and Prejudice* tonight."

I smother a groan but do remember agreeing to that plan before I realized there was a party happening next door. I'm not even cool enough to know about parties, let alone be invited.

"Five more minutes."

"Fine. I'll make popcorn." Her voice moves away from the tree house. "If you aren't inside when I hit play, you're on trash duty for the rest of the month."

"Yeah, yeah. I'll be there." The wind blows my hair around my face. I untie the flannel shirt from my waist and slip it on, then hug my knees to my chest and drop my chin to rest on my arm.

Three months ago, I moved in next door to the hottest party spot at college with Violet and two other friends, Jane and Dahlia.

The White House, as it's called, is aptly named, not only because of its size and color but because the epic parties thrown here are the college version of being asked to dine with dignitaries or royalty. Or, I'm guessing, since the closest I've come to attending a party there is watching from my favorite nook on the other side of the property line.

The starting lineup for the university's men's basketball team lives next door, but it's an all-inclusive place to be for the elite population on campus—members of Greek life, jocks of the top sports, stunningly gorgeous girls, and *him*.

Liam Price—hockey player, junior, engineering major.

We have a physics class together this semester, so I know the tilt of his shoulders as he leans back in his seat, the way he chews on the end of his pen when he's thinking, and that his friends sometimes call him Dreamboat as a way to tease him about his neatly styled blond hair and preppy clothes.

Tonight he's sitting with his teammates on the side of the patio closest to me. The guys he's with are drinking one cup of foamy beer after another, but not Liam. Like many other nights I've watched him, he holds a water bottle in one hand. He laughs and talks along with his buddies, but as they get drunk and loud, his calm and put-together presence never wavers.

My pulse races as a pretty girl approaches his circle of friends. The way she waltzes up to a group of guys with such confidence and ease is truly inspiring. He unfolds his tall frame, offering his seat to the newcomer. She smiles and places a hand on his forearm, then gushes something I can't hear over the party noise before taking his chair.

Did I mention he's a gentleman?

He drains the rest of his water and looks around the party. Sometimes I think he doesn't feel like he fits in either. Still, he's on that side of the fence.

My breath hitches when his gaze lifts to the tree house across the property line, but as soon as I think he's seen me, his stare continues on.

Invisibility is my superpower. Except I can't turn it off. For three months, he's looked in my direction without seeing me.

"Daisy!" Violet yells from the back door. I'd take the trash out every month until the end of time if I thought sitting up here and studying my popular peers would get me any closer to being one of them.

With a sigh, I take one last longing look at everything I'm missing out on and then start down the ladder. My Saturday night plans include watching Colin Firth as Mr. Darcy for at least the third time this semester. Violet has a thing for Austen, and I have a thing for romance and optimism, so I don't mind so much. I prefer the Matthew Macfadyen version, though.

Before I moved next door, I might have even been excited to quote our favorite lines and swoon as Darcy falls for Elizabeth. Back then, it was easy to write off these parties like I wasn't missing anything, but now…

Now, as I enter the quaint and quiet stone house practically hidden next to the massive one next door, I wonder, what would it take for a campus wallflower to climb the fence and be seen?

1

DAISY

"I'm late," Dahlia calls as she hurries down the stairs with an apple in one hand and her golf bag slung over her shoulder. She puts the apple in her mouth to wave and then flings open the door. A breeze flows through the living room as she slams the door behind her and jogs across the street, joining more student athletes on their way to practice.

Our house is only a few blocks from campus, nestled between dorms on the southside and Ray Fieldhouse and the rest of the athletic facilities.

Weekday afternoons are the best for people watching.

"I haven't seen any baseball players in their cute pants," Violet says, looking over my shoulder.

"They have a day off. I heard a guy in class talking about it." Jane flips through a Cosmopolitan magazine on the couch. She looks up from the page and pulls back the curtain giving us a better view.

Basketball players jog the street, football players are heading in for weight training in cut-off T-shirts, and if I squint, I can just make out the empty baseball diamond in the distance. The hockey arena is two blocks west and out of view, but I like to picture Liam at practice in all that padding, flashing that big, bright smile underneath his helmet.

The prick of a needle on my shoulder makes me jump.

"Hold still. I'm almost done." Only Violet could sound annoyed and sympathetic at the same time.

As instructed, I stand perfectly still while she uses me as a model for her latest creation. The material falls to the floor with a small train. The bodice is a black corset that squeezes my ribs and pushes up my small boobs to an impressive, gravity-defying height. Soft, see-through lace covers my shoulders and arms, and clasps at my neck with a vintage brooch. The cropped blouse does nothing to cover my cleavage, but I'm certain that's the point.

The dress is Victorian Gothic with a sexy edge. Very Violet. She's studying fashion design, and her affinity for all things historical comes through loud and clear with everything she creates.

Violet places a pair of stilettos in front of me and then sits to do the bottom hem.

"Wouldn't it be better if you pinned it with me flat footed? That way you'll be able to wear two or three-inch heels, no problem." My cousin is a good two inches shorter than me and has a propensity for heels, whereas I prefer to keep both feet firmly planted on the ground.

She shakes her head, black hair swishing around her shoulders with the small movement. I step awkwardly into Violet's hot pink stilettos. Her feet are a half-size smaller and pinch my toes. It's a good thing the only thing I need to do in these is stand.

Violet removes a pin from the cushion around her wrist and secures the fabric at the top of my foot. I force myself not to fidget. We've been at this for the better part of an hour, and Violet isn't much company as she works. She is deep in concentration, and any words she speaks as she makes her way around me, pinning the material in place, are to instruct me or comment on the people outside. And Jane spends her entire break between classes reading through the dozens of magazines she subscribes to—physical and digital.

"Okay." Violet stands and does another circle around me. "What do you think?"

"It's gorgeous, as always. What's it for?" I step out of the heels, thankful to feel my toes again.

When Violet grins, her entire face lights up with excitement. "It's for the Wallflower Ball in January."

My shock of her creating another dress for the event (this would be number three she's designed and made for the ball) is temporarily blinded by her nickname for the masquerade party she's putting together. "Can we stop calling it that?"

In a flash, her smile falls into an annoyed frown. "Wallflowers are awesome. Own it."

Oh, I'm owning it. Not like I have a choice. That's one of many differences between Violet and me. She's friendly and outgoing. People are always quick to like her. She did the dance team in high school and, she'd kill me for telling anyone, was even the homecoming queen. Two months into our freshman year at Valley, she just gave it all up and decided she was over partying and hanging with vapid, self-loathing assholes. Those are definitely words straight from her mouth.

"What's wrong with the last two you made for the ball?" I smooth my hand down the lace skirt. I can't get over how soft it feels.

"Nothing. This one is for you." Her smile is locked back in place. She pulls out her phone and snaps a picture of me, all while I still process her words.

"I can't wear this."

"You can." She moves to stand beside me and holds out the screen of her phone to show me the photo she took. "It's perfect."

The dress *is* perfect. I hardly recognize myself from the neck down. I'm far more comfortable in my own clothes, not because I don't love this but because it's far too beautiful for me.

I glance at my stunning cousin. Our fathers are brothers, but our personalities are as different as the way we look. My hair is the color of wet sand, and my blue eyes are nothing special. I'm average height and just... well, average. Violet, on the other hand, inherited her mother's Korean genes. Her long hair is a soft black, and her eyes are a dark brown that lighten when she laughs.

I love my cousin, but she doesn't always understand what it's like to be the shy, quiet girl.

"Do you not like it?" Uncertainty tugs her brows down as she searches my face. Sometimes I forget that Violet has insecurities. It doesn't make any sense to me because she's so good at everything she does.

"Are you kidding me? I feel like a harlot."

She still stares at me with big, unsure eyes.

"That was a compliment. I've never felt more beautiful, Vi. I'm just not sure it's me."

"You could be a harlot. You'd just have to speak to your crushes instead of watching them from the tree house." This from Jane, who puts the magazine down and comes to stand in front of me. "You look beautiful, Daisy."

I appreciate their confidence in me, however unfounded. I have a pretty good idea of how it'd go if I actually spoke to Liam, and it doesn't end up with me wearing this dress on a date where he pulls me into the corner and ravishes me because he just can't wait another minute to have me. The dress is good. It isn't *that* good.

Violet's lips pull up at the corners, and she squeezes me from the side. "It's going to be great this year." She moves to unzip me. "Did I tell you that I was able to book the big ballroom in the Moreno building? And Jane's parents donated tablecloths and these gorgeous candle centerpieces." She looks at our roommate. "Thanks again for that."

"No problem." Jane sits back on the couch and picks up her magazine.

"Wow. That's quite a step up from last year's little shindig in the dorm lounge." We had flat soda in Solo cups, and the lighting was fluorescent.

Violet first had the idea for a masquerade ball when we were living in the dorms last year. Her roommate was off to some sorority formal, and we were both pining over how there weren't big social events for people like us who didn't rush Greek life or date guys popular enough to be invited to them. So, we organized one, or Violet did.

"Yes, it's gotten a little out of hand." She shrugs through an excited smile that tells me it's going to be way, way over the top.

"How can I help?" I ask.

"Could you take care of the flowers? The florist up the street already has us on her schedule, but I need to give her specifics."

"Flowers?"

"Yes, flowers." She cuts me a look. "It's the *Wallflower* Ball."

A groan slips past my lips. "You really have to stop calling it that."

"I'll text you all the details. Are you sure you can do it? The whole concept revolves around the flowers. They're doing an arch and..." She trails off when it's clear I'm only half-listening. "Don't forget."

"I will go this week."

"Thank you."

She takes the dress from me, and I pull on my far-less-stylish one and boots.

"I'm off to class." My pulse jumps because I'm going to see Liam in fifteen minutes.

My roommates grin. They know how much I look forward to this class twice a week.

"Say hi to Liam for us," Jane teases.

Not likely.

2

DAISY

Our physics professor is a short, bald man with a booming voice and a quick smile. He spends the two-hour lab pacing the front of the room and trying with all his might to get us pumped about our work. He's great. Friendly, a little quirky, and a whole lot animated. He teaches with his whole body, hands waving wildly as he gives us instructions for today's assignment.

But despite his best efforts, my attention is pulled to the guy sitting at the table in front of me. Today Liam wears a black polo shirt with jeans. His blond hair is covered by a matching black baseball cap. Even when he's casual, he's put together. He leans on his left elbow, pen poised against his full lips, giving our boisterous professor his entire focus.

He's a direct contradiction to the guy next to him. Jordan Thatcher's messy black hair curls around a backward hat that says *I heart MILFs*. His shirt is wrinkled, and his socks don't match. He's handsome if you don't mind that *I just finished practice and couldn't be bothered to find clean clothes* look.

Liam and Jordan are teammates, but they're so different I don't understand how they're friends off the ice. While Liam is known for being a good guy, Jordan's reputation is less pristine. If there's a party, he's there. Girls love his carefree, party-hard attitude. I find it... daunting. Sure, I'd love to care a little less and break out of my shell, but Jordan doesn't seem like he cares about anything.

His head is bowed over his desk, and he scribbles furiously like he's taking down every word Professor Green says. Except even from my table behind him, I can see what he's really doing is coloring in the block letters of the notebook brand on the front.

When the professor has finished and given us the go-ahead to start, I sigh and glance at the empty chair next to me. It's the third week in a row that my lab partner has been a no-show. She's either dropped or on her way to failing.

I read through the instructions that I partially missed while staring at Liam. He and Jordan always walk in at the last second, so it really isn't my fault that I need the first few minutes of class to scope him out.

I pull my hair back into a ponytail as Liam stands in front of his stool. He's tall, and his broad shoulders pull the fabric of his shirt as he leans over to scribble something on a piece of paper. His partner is less enthusiastic, sitting and watching as Liam gets them started.

Blowing out a breath, I drop my gaze back to my own desk. I like physics, but this is going to be a lot to get through on my own.

"Miss Johnson." Professor Green approaches my table as I'm re-reading the first steps of the lab. He clicks his tongue, hand on his hip as he looks at the empty space beside me. "Your partner is missing again."

I offer an awkward smile.

"These labs are really meant for two." He opens his stance and stares down his nose at the classroom. My pulse thrums quickly as he weighs his options. Every other table is paired up. It'll be just my luck that he'll decide to be my partner or stick me with a group that ignores me and continues in their happy twosome. I hate this kind of attention. It's like walking into a room full of people or being called on in class. My skin itches and I twist my hands in front of me.

It feels like everyone is avoiding looking up from their table because they know Professor Green is searching for somewhere to place me. It's irrational. I know this. Most of them probably don't even realize what's happening. It isn't like they notice me any other time, so why would now be different? Still, I hate the thought of being added to a group that doesn't want me.

"Let's put you with Mr. Price and Mr. Thatcher."

My heart drops into my stomach. Frozen, I don't speak or move while Professor Green steps closer to Liam and Jordan with a pleased smile at his problem-solving.

"Miss Johnson will be joining you until her partner returns," he tells them.

To my horror, Liam looks around, completely clueless about who Miss Johnson is.

It's me, you idiot, I scream in my head, then silently apologize because it isn't his fault I've never once worked up the courage to speak to him. Actually, that isn't true. Once, I sneezed, and he said, "Bless You," and I thanked him.

Jordan and Liam finally locate the only unpartnered person in the class. Liam's eyes widen in an observing sort of way as he stares at me. He lifts a hand in a polite wave. Jordan scoots his stool over with a loud screech against the tile floor.

I scoop up my belongings, and on rubber legs, I move the eight feet from my table to theirs.

"Hi, I'm Liam." He moves into the middle spot behind the table and offers me his chair. "This is Jordan."

He leans back slightly so I can see Jordan on the other side of him.

I nod to each of them.

"I didn't catch your first name," Liam says. "Unless you want us to call you Miss Johnson."

"Dai-sy." My voice shakes on both syllables.

His smile sets free a thousand butterflies inside of me. This close, he seems so much taller.

"Cool. Nice to meet you, Daisy. We were just about to trace the rays of the concave lens. Do you want to do the honors?"

Jordan snorts. "Honors?"

Liam ignores him and flips on the light on the projector. Rays of light stretch out onto the paper. I'm still partially frozen.

"Need a pencil?" He lifts his from the top of his notebook, and because I'm not sure where mine is at the moment, I accept it.

My hand shakes as I trace along the rays with a ruler. I'm embarrassed to admit how his presence a mere foot away from me has me unsteady on my feet and struggling to make air flow through my lungs.

The daisy charm on my necklace swings forward as I crouch over the table. Liam drums his thumbs absently on the table.

"There," I say when I'm done.

I finally get a deep breath that clears some of my nerves, but then I get a big inhale of his faint cologne, and my chest tightens. He even smells perfect.

Liam looks to Jordan. "What's next?"

Jordan stays sitting on his stool while Liam and I finish marking the paper. Every step, Liam checks with him, and then the two of us complete it. I can tell it's how they always do things, and it doesn't surprise me that Liam has been doing the brunt of the work.

While Liam reads through the next step in our assignment, I take the opportunity to stare at him up close. His brows tug together in concentration, and the tip of his tongue pushes between his teeth. He has great bone structure, high cheekbones, and a long, straight nose. He's clean-shaven, and his skin has warm undertones that make his blond hair and blue eyes contrast nicely.

I feel Jordan's gaze on me. When I meet his dark stare, a humored smile curves his lips. Blushing at being caught checking out his friend, I fidget with my necklace and look around at the other tables while Liam finishes.

"So, Daisy." Liam's voice brings me back. "What's your major?"

"Physics," I say automatically in the practiced response I've honed, and then I add, "and art. Physics and art."

A slow smile lifts the corners of his mouth. His forehead crinkles as his brows raise in surprise. "Double major?"

I wet my lips and nod. A few seconds pass before I realize the polite thing to do is ask him the same question back, even if I already know the answer.

"What about you?"

"Civil engineering." He pokes his pencil toward Jordan. "Both of us."

I refuse to look at Jordan again, but I aim a smile between them.

After thirty minutes, my anxiety finally abates enough that I find my voice.

"You play hockey, right?"

"Yeah." Liam beams at me. "How'd you know."

I point to Jordan's Valley U hockey T-shirt.

"Right. Have you been to a game?"

"No," I admit, now wishing I hadn't brought it up.

"What? Never? What year are you?"

"Sophomore."

He shakes his head and shoots me a playful smile. "You're missing out. We're pretty good."

He's being modest. They won the Frozen Four two years ago, and last year got pretty close to going back to the national tournament.

Jordan, who's stayed quiet except for reading instructions, speaks up, "Don't bother, man. It doesn't really seem like her kind of thing."

He does a quick and dismissive once-over of my dress and boots. At five foot four, I'm slightly shorter than average, and my small bone structure makes me look younger and smaller than I am. I probably won't be strapping on pads anytime soon, but violence in of itself doesn't bother me. Though admittedly, I don't completely understand why anyone thought it was a good idea to put a bunch of guys on ice skates and give them sticks and permission to ram into one another.

"It is," I protest.

"Yeah?" Jordan grins. "My mistake. Who is your favorite hockey player?"

My cheeks heat with embarrassment.

"Home games are the best," Liam ignores him, leaning forward and blocking Jordan from my view. "The roar of the crowd and excitement is like a big party. You should come sometime and see for yourself."

"Yeah, maybe."

I don't really know why I haven't gone before. It's just one more thing I've passed on for safer, quieter options. Plus, Violet has sworn off sporting events unless it's for Dahlia, and all my friends are friends with her.

The rest of the class passes with more small talk, and the three of us finish the assignment before anyone else.

"We work well together," Liam says as he hooks his backpack over one shoulder.

"Yeah," I agree a little breathlessly. My heart races like it did earlier. "Thanks for letting me join."

"Of course. Have a good day, Daisy."

I suck in a breath at my name on his lips.

"You too, Liam," I chirp back.

Jordan hangs back a second, and when I don't say anything, he chuckles. "Yeah, great. I'll have a good day too."

I speed walk to the café to meet Violet. She's already sitting with a coffee, her sketchbook in front of her. When she sees me, she looks up and breaks a smile.

"What happened? You look way too happy."

"I talked to him."

"Who?"

"Liam." I pace in front of her, waving my hands wildly. "And he talked to me. Like a lot. He was so nice, Violet. Like not just polite, but friendly. He asked me questions, and he invited me to come to a hockey game." Or maybe he just said I should go to a game. Whatever. It's as close to an invite as I'm ever getting.

"Whoa. Seriously?"

I nod my head quickly like a bobblehead.

"Oh my gosh. I can't believe it. What spurred you to do it? Was it all the *Pride and Prejudice*? Women knew how to speak to dudes back then—cut them with words without even trying." Her eyes widen. "Ooooh, or was it the dress?"

"My lab partner was absent again, and I got moved to their group."

"Their?"

"Liam and Jordan," I grumble the second name a little. It would have been a perfect two hours if it weren't for him.

"Ah, the bad boy to your good guy crush." She takes a bite of her sandwich. "One of them is faking."

"I don't think it's Jordan."

"Then maybe Liam isn't really that nice."

"He is, Vi." I finally sit and remember dreamily how considerate he was. No one else would have welcomed me into their group like that. He was everything I hoped he would be. No, even more.

"All right, if you say so." Violet leans her elbows on the table. "You finally talked to him. Now what?"

Now what, indeed.

3

JORDAN

THE MOOD in the locker room is thick with frustration. My shoulder blades rest against the back of the wooden stall, and my breathing still comes in quick, ragged gulps. Sweat pours down my face. I haven't moved yet, but I can already feel the burn of my muscles in my quads.

"Fuck me. That was brutal." Even talking is painful.

Liam grunts beside me. He hunches over, elbows on his knees and a towel draped over his head. A glance around at the rest of the team tells me everyone is hurting as bad as we are.

It's a month into the season, and we look like shit. We only lost two guys to graduation and transfers at the end of last year, but our conference champ record is taunting us as we struggle to put the puck in the net. Coach decided we needed a little motivation in the form of skating our asses off for two hours.

My buddy curls up into a sitting position and lets out a long breath that puffs out his cheeks. "Wanna grab a beer at The Hideout?"

"Can't. I have to finish that paper for tech writing."

"You still haven't done that?" The disbelieving grin he tosses my way doesn't have any judgment in it. "I thought you were doing that last night when I crashed early."

"Nah. I ended up playing video games with the guys across the hall. Then some girls from the volleyball team brought up a bottle of Malibu."

"That explains the high-pitched noises coming from your bedroom when I got up to shower this morning. I thought you were singing along to Celine Dion again."

"Hey, Celine's got great pipes. So did Abby, or was it Anna?"

He gives his head a playful shake and then gets to his feet. "Finish it and then meet up with us." Liam struggles to get his practice jersey over his head. We all look like we took a dip in the swimming pool after practice without removing our gear.

"I thought you said *a* beer?" He hardly ever drinks, especially during the week.

"It feels like a pitcher kind of night."

No freaking shit. "Doubt I'll make it but call me if you need a ride."

He tosses his jersey in the laundry bin. "I'm not staying out that late. I'll be home before you finish that paper, probably."

I snort a laugh. "Later."

Back at the dorms, I pull a half-eaten sandwich and a blue Powerade from the mini-fridge and sit at my desk. I scarf down the food while I pull up the document due tomorrow.

One sentence—that's how much I've written on the three-to-five-page paper assigned two weeks ago. Damn. I knew I was going to regret putting it off as long as I did.

I turn on some music and twirl in my desk chair, hoping an idea comes to me. I can bullshit for three pages no problem, but I need some inspiration.

A knock at our suite door snatches my attention, and I shoot up, glad for a distraction.

"Leonard," I say as I pull the door wide. "What's up?"

Stepping back, I give him room to duck his head to enter. At six foot six, Gavin Leonard's a good five inches taller than me and towers over the general population.

"Where's Price?" he asks.

"He and some of the guys went out after practice."

"And you stayed in?" He scans the suite I share with Liam, his gaze stopping on my open bedroom door. His voice drops to a whisper. "You got a girl in there?"

"Do you really think I'd be answering the door for your Gumby ass if I did?" I take a seat on the couch, and he drops into the chair. "What are you doing slumming it with us dorm-folk?"

He leans back with a smirk. Gavin lives at The White House with three other basketball players. It's a palace. They have their own gym, pool, and media room. Must be freaking nice.

"Warren lives downstairs," he says of one of his teammates.

"Uh-oh. What'd he do to deserve a visit from the team captain?"

A devious smile pulls at his lips. "Today's his birthday. The guys took him out to dinner, and we filled every inch of floor in his room with cups of water for when he comes back."

I bark a laugh at the image.

"For real," he says. "What are you doing tonight? There's a party at Sigma and a bunch of people at The Hideout."

I rake a hand through my hair. "I have a paper due tomorrow."

"So finish it and let's go out. I'm meeting the guys in twenty."

Indecision wars inside of me. "I shouldn't. Practices have been awful, the team isn't meshing, and we have a game on Friday."

"Staying in while the rest of your guys are out isn't going to magically make it come together."

He's probably not wrong about that. Still, I hesitate.

"What time is your first class tomorrow?" he asks.

"One I'm actually planning on attending?" I ask with a laugh. "Not until one."

"Practice or workouts?"

I shake my head. Coach gave us the morning off to recover from the brutal conditioning we did today.

He stands tall. "What are we even talking about then? Come on. At least come say happy birthday to Warren, and then you can come back and finish it and still get a full eight hours of beauty sleep in."

"Yeah, of course." I stand. Warren came out for my twenty-first celebration. It'd be shitty not to go and at least have one beer with him.

When we walk up to Sigma, the scene is insane. I can barely see the front door with all the people standing in the front yard. And the party is in the back.

"Whoa," I say as adrenaline hits. I love a good party.

"I told you." Gavin pushes at my shoulder and stretches his long legs to hurry up to the house.

I texted Liam on the way to see if he wanted to meet up with us, but he was already headed back to the dorm. *Be like Liam*, I tell myself. One beer, and I'm out.

A BOOMING VOICE cuts through the silence, and the ground beneath me shakes. "Gotta get up, man. Class in twenty."

"Unnggh." My mouth is dry, and my head splinters in two when I open my eyes.

Liam's amused smile greets me. "You look like shit. I thought you were taking it easy last night."

I pull myself up and crack my neck to work out a kink. "Sigma was crazy. Biggest after hours I've seen all semester."

I reach for the water bottle on my nightstand. One beer turned into two or three, and then several rounds of birthday shots.

"The Hideout was packed last night too." He backs out of my room, stopping in the doorway. "Did you finish your paper?"

Ah fuck. I had my alarm set for eight this morning to get up and finish it, but I must have turned it off and passed right back out. Not surprising since I didn't crash until almost three.

My face must give him the answer because he laughs. "Bring it to lab. You can work on it there."

"Thank you."

I have just enough time to shower and grab my shit before we head off to the Emerson Building for our physics lab. I'm finishing off a bag of chips when we walk in. Dr. Green pauses his lecture and waits for us to take our seats.

For twenty minutes, he talks, giving us all the relevant information for today's lab. My grades are decent. I pull Bs and Cs, thanks in large part to sharing most of my classes with Liam. He keeps me in check with school, and I like to think I've helped him learn to cut loose a little. Freshman year, when we got to Valley, he'd never had a drop of alcohol, and he spent every night studying.

I'm not saying there's anything wrong with either of those things, but it's college—you have to live a little.

When Dr. Green finishes, Liam nods toward my bag on the floor. "We've got this. Just make it look like you're feverishly taking notes."

"We?"

At my question, Daisy steps up to our table. She pushes a lock of dark blonde hair behind one ear. "Hi."

"Stuck with us again, huh?" Liam asks, shooting her a charming grin.

She eats it right up, dropping her gaze to the floor with a smile. "Yeah. My partner must have dropped the class."

Liam grabs an extra stool and sets it next to her. "You're our partner now."

"Thank you." She moves like a scared rabbit, perching herself on the very edge of the seat. I'm not sure I'd heard her say a single word all semester that wasn't a direct response to a question until two days ago when Dr. Green put her in our group. She's smart, though. Our professor always calls on her when no one else knows the answer.

She's pretty cute. The shy, quiet thing she has going on is a whole vibe.

My buddy is into it, too. I can tell. They're perfect for one another: Barbie and Ken, brainy, introvert edition. Liam's a good guy, the best, actually. If anyone can make her feel at ease, it's him. That's probably why Dr. Green put her at our table.

"How should we break up the work?" she asks as she leans

forward and reads the lab handout. Her nails are painted a bright, fiery red. That makes me smile. They're so much bolder than anything else about her.

"It's just you and me today," Liam says and tilts his head toward me. "Jordan needs to finish a paper. Is that cool?"

Her gaze slides over to me briefly, not meeting mine before she pins another shy smile at Liam. "Perfect."

As planned, I start on my paper while the two of them work on the lab. I sneak a glance at them huddled together, smiling and laughing like physics is a freaking blast. Her cheeks are pink with a flush, and she looks at Liam like he's the freaking moon and stars.

I'm closing in on three pages and reading over it again to check for errors when they finish the lab.

"Done?" Liam asks me as they clean up the lab supplies.

"Yeah. I just need a closing sentence to wrap it up."

"What's the paper about?" Daisy's voice almost blends in with the noise of the classroom. She's so quiet, but she's talking a little more today.

"Time management." Liam snorts as he responds for me. Okay, it's kind of funny. Still, I glare at him.

"You had to write a paper on time management? For what class?"

"Technical writing. It's tips and tricks, that kind of thing. We drew out of a hat for topics."

She nods slowly. "Maybe you should end it with a cautionary tale of what happens when you don't have good time management, and you have to finish assignments during other classes."

Liam chuckles softly. Damn, is this girl burning me?

"Maybe I was sick yesterday or at a funeral."

"Were you?"

I huff a laugh and grin at her. "No."

The three of us pack up to leave. Liam has to haul ass across campus to meet with his adviser, but I take my time and walk out with Daisy. Even the way she moves is gentle and unassuming. She side-eyes me when I fall into step beside her.

"Thanks for today. I'm sorry you had to pick up my slack."

She regards me carefully, like she isn't sure if I'm being genuine or not. I don't even know why I'm apologizing. They still finished early, even without my help.

I get the briefest of nods from her, and she takes another tentative step down the hall.

"Are you coming to the game tomorrow night?"

"Oh, umm…" She has this habit of tucking her hair behind her right ear, and she does it again now. "I'm not sure."

"A big hockey fan like you?" I tease.

She blushes again but doesn't say anything.

We come to the outside door, and I hold it open for her. The wind whips her long hair around her head, sending the strands and their fruity smell into my face.

She looks over her shoulder as she corrals her wild hair.

"I'm going that way." I jab my thumb in the opposite direction toward my tech writing class. "Are you heading to another class?"

"No, I'm done for the day."

"Are you in the dorms?"

She hesitates like she's confused why I'm asking so many questions. Me too, but I find her sort of fascinating. "No, I live off-campus."

"Huh."

She looks at me quizzically. I can hardly tell her I find that surprising even though I do.

"You shouldn't spend so much time socializing between classes."

"What's that?" Now it's my turn to be confused.

A ghost of a smile crosses her pink lips. "It's another tip for better time management."

4

JORDAN

"I thought you two had forgotten." Gavin tosses a wad of material at me. "New shirts."

"Sorry. Coach held us late again." Liam sets his bowling shoes down on the floor and takes a seat. "Just the three of us tonight?"

Gavin nods. "Jenkins had a study session."

I hand Liam a shirt and hold up mine in front of me, then drop it to look at Gavin. "Lucky Strikes?"

He stands and picks up his blue bowling ball. "We couldn't be Team Blue Balls again this year."

"Why not?" I ask and slip the black Dickies shirt with our new team name printed on the front over my T-shirt. "It's funny."

"It's really not that funny," Liam says.

I flip him off as he moves to the computer.

"Same order?" he asks as he punches in our names.

"Sounds good to me."

I'm rusty from not playing for a few months. The three of us, plus Gavin's teammate, Andy Jenkins, joined a bowling league freshman year when Gavin and Andy lived across the hall instead of their sweet new digs at The White House. We were bored and heard this place never carded for alcohol. At the time, it seemed like as good a reason as any to join a bowling league. But two years later, we're still doing it even after we've all turned twenty-one except Gavin.

At the end of the first game, we pause to grab a pitcher of beer and shoot the shit.

I stretch out my legs in front of me and rub at my left quad. "Coach is gonna kill us if he keeps running us like he has the past two weeks."

"Practice is still that bad?" Gavin asks as he fills our glasses. Liam waves him off in favor of his water.

"It's pretty bad. Coach doesn't know whether to keep yelling or give us the world's longest pep talk," I say.

We lost another game last weekend. There is nothing worse than losing at home.

"What's the problem? Are the rookies struggling that much to mesh with the rest of the team?" Gavin's question is innocent enough, but I feel the prickle of discomfort wash over my buddy.

"I'm going to get some air." Liam starts toward the doors without pausing for our response.

Gavin waits until he's out of earshot. "Did I say something wrong?"

"Nah. It isn't you. He's feeling the pressure." Coach made Liam captain this year, and ever since, his game on the ice has gone downhill.

"Is it just hockey, or does he have other distractions?"

"Like?"

"I don't know. A tough class schedule?"

I shake my head. "He has straight A's."

"New girlfriend?"

"No." Another shake.

"Good," he says. "Nothing like a new chick to make a guy lose focus. Trust me on that. New girlfriends are the worst kind of distraction. Women weaken the legs."

"What?" I bust a laugh at his last words.

"It's from *Rocky*."

I keep staring at him.

He jumps up and hops from leg to leg, tossing punches like a boxer. "The movie. *Rocky*?"

"Oh, I understood the first time, but don't stop making an ass out of yourself on my account."

He stops and flips me off.

THE NEXT AFTERNOON, Liam shows up late for practice. His face is red, and his shoulders are stiff.

"Sorry, Coach," he says as he skates onto the ice.

He's never been late for practice or a workout. Never.

I fall into line behind him for drills. "Is everything okay?"

"Yeah." He stares straight ahead, jaw set.

I stop him with a glove to his bicep before he can skate forward. "Are you sick?"

"I'm fine. I overslept. No big deal."

I let him go, but now I'm more worried than before. He wasn't in his room when I left. I know because I checked. I needed a clean pair of shorts. But why the hell would he lie?

At the end of practice, Coach stops him.

"Price. Do you want to tell me why you were late today?" Instead of waiting for his answer, he continues. "You're late, you're missing passes, you're slow on your feet. If you keep it up, you're going to find yourself next to me during games."

"It was my fault." My chest heaves as I struggle to catch my breath. "I shut off his alarm before I left. I thought he was up."

Coach's mouth falls into a hard line.

"It won't happen again," Liam promises.

"Good." Coach motions with his head toward the locker room. "Get out of here."

When we sit in our stalls, my buddy finally speaks. "Thanks."

"Where were you?"

"I told you. I overslept."

"I know you weren't in your room."

His brows pull up toward the blond, matted hair on his forehead. "Checking up on me?"

"I forgot to do laundry again," I admit. I pull the band of my hockey pants down to show him the shorts I borrowed.

He chuckles lightly. "I was in the library. I passed out with my head on the desk trying to look over econ notes."

"I should have known."

Despite the lousy practice, Liam seems to be in a better mood when we get back to the dorms. I'm playing video games, and he brings his laptop out to the living room to work on an assignment.

"I'm thinking of asking out our lab partner," he says without looking up from the screen.

"Who?"

"Daisy. The girl in our physics lab."

"Right." I ponder that, not liking how it sits with me. "Really?"

"She's nice."

I pause the game. Liam hasn't really dated in the three years I've known him. He hooks up so infrequently it still surprises me when I wake up to find him walking a girl out. But something tells me him asking out Daisy wouldn't be like that. It'd be real. They'd go on actual dates and shit.

"Won't that be weird if shit goes south, and we have to team up with her twice a week for class?"

"Look at you all glass half empty."

"I'm just saying, maybe now isn't the best time to start something."

The insinuation is clear, and he pulls his bottom lip behind his teeth and bobs his head. "Yeah. You might be right about that. I'm one screw up away from Coach benching me."

"Of course, I'm right. When have I ever steered you wrong?"

He cocks a brow.

"Okay, yeah. Don't answer that, but dating is distracting. You can trust me on that."

"And partying and hooking up four or five nights a week isn't?"

"You're not me. You have to ease into being as awesome as me. Maybe try getting a polite hand job at a party or something first."

THURSDAY, during our physics lab, Daisy joins our table again. She and Liam fall into easy conversation, and I take my usual role, reading through the steps and calling them out. It's how Liam and I always worked. I learn better by writing things down, and he's a hands-on guy.

A pit forms in my stomach as I watch my lab partners interact.

Liam would never intentionally sabotage the team. He's too good of a guy for that, but the way Daisy is looking at him with hearts in her eyes sends warning bells off in my head. She isn't the kind of girl you take out once, hook up, and then maybe call for a repeat a few times in the future when your schedule is clear.

Daisy is the kind of girl that would have someone like Liam wrapped around her little pinky finger. She's the perfect sweet, smart, naïve catnip for him.

We're doing a projectile motion lab that involves launching a ball onto carbon paper. It's an easy lab, and as Liam loads up the ball in the launcher, Daisy smiles and moves the carbon paper a few feet away, which brings her closer to me.

"It's probably easier if I sit in the middle," I say.

She hesitates, then looks between Liam and me.

"I can walk around to the other side of the table," she says.

I fight a smile. She wants to be near him. How cute.

"You know what." I drop my pencil. "Give me a turn on that thing."

On my feet, I step toward Liam and the launcher.

"Yeah?" he asks with an apprehensive smirk.

"Looks fun." It absolutely doesn't.

He tosses the silver ball at me and takes my seat.

Since I've read the handout, I'm already adjusting the angle to thirty degrees and preparing to fire when Liam gives me the instruction.

"Ready?" I ask Daisy.

Her blue eyes flit over me through the safety goggles, and she pushes them up higher on her nose.

The ball shoots out and bounces onto the paper, then directly at her. She tries to catch it, misses, and a series of metallic pings ring out as it bounces along the floor.

Her cheeks are pink as she circles, trying to capture it. Liam and I both move to action. He gets there first, snatching it up and holding it out for her. He winks. On anyone else, it would seem like a skeevy move, but he pulls it off, and Daisy swoons at his feet.

"Why don't you have a turn?" I motion toward the launcher.

She nods and moves into position behind it. I stand near the paper, ready to catch the ball after it lands.

Her blonde hair falls forward like a curtain blocking half of her face as she leans down to set the ball in place. She glances up at me, or in my general direction anyway, before she fires. I nod, giving her the go-ahead. As the ball comes my way, I'm temporarily distracted as her shirt gapes hinting at a little cleavage. The daisy charm around her neck dangles seductively. Her boobs are small, but the cleavage is still nice.

The ball bounces while I'm still staring, but I easily catch it in one hand. She stands tall and takes a tentative step toward me like she wants to switch spots again.

"Nah, you go again," I say and hold the ball up to indicate I'm going to toss it to her. She places both hands out in front of her apprehensively. I smother a laugh and throw it directly into her hands.

I'd be lying if I said I didn't look down her shirt the next three times she does it, but I convince myself it's better this way, so she doesn't fumble around trying to catch the ball as it shoots out at her. And I think she kind of likes sending flying objects in my direction.

When we're finished with the launcher and start calculating

velocity, I find myself back on my side, and the two of them huddled together.

I keep waiting for my buddy to ask her out, but he doesn't even after we finish the lab and start packing up to leave. Huh. Maybe he wasn't that serious about it. Or maybe I'm just that good.

Or he caught sight of her small tits or terrible ball catching skills and decided against it. It doesn't sound like him, but whatever. I'm just thankful he didn't.

Crisis adverted.

5

DAISY

OVER THE NEXT TWO WEEKS, I continue to sit with Liam and Jordan during physics, and it actually starts to feel normal. Or as normal as sitting next to your popular crush while trying not to physically combust ever feels.

Sometimes the way he smiles at me, I convince myself that he likes me too. But when class is over, he says goodbye and races out the door like he can't wait to get wherever he's going.

Today when I slide into the chair next to Liam, he gives me the same smile and greeting, but his face doesn't light up the same way, and he drops his gaze to the table while Professor Green talks through the lab.

While we work through the lab, he barely speaks—even to Jordan. I've never seen Liam like this. He's sullen, broody even. He ducks out to refill his water bottle halfway through, and Jordan scoots closer.

"The next step is to measure the amplitude." He taps his pencil on the paper.

I nod, then ask, "Is he okay?"

"Yeah," he says as he hitches the sleeve of his T-shirt up on his shoulder. The movement lifts the cuff showing off his bicep and the bottom of a tattoo. He has a few. A long, skinny cross on the back of his left arm, then a hockey player and a puck going into a net—one on each thigh, that I've seen on days when he has worn shorts. Today his jeans cover them, and I imagine he has even more ink hidden underneath his clothes.

"He doesn't seem okay."

"Just a tough practice today."

"Oh." My brows knit in confusion. I expected something, I don't know, bigger? "That's all?"

"Were you hoping for more? Maybe a dead pet or incurable disease?"

"No, of course not." My face heats.

He grins and brings his pencil up behind one ear.

"You were at practice too?"

His dark brows pull together slightly as he nods.

"And yet you haven't lost your sparkle."

His deep chuckle does something funny to my stomach. "Part of my charm, I guess. I don't let things get to me like Liam does."

I finish the measurement before I prod a little more. I want to understand Liam—what makes him tick and what gets to him. "A bad practice really gets him that upset?"

"Sometimes, yeah," he says.

My face must show my surprise because Jordan shakes his head. "I wouldn't expect you to understand."

I start to ask what he means, but Liam returns, and Jordan moves back to his spot. The time to himself seems to have done Liam well. He smiles a little brighter as he takes his seat and sets his bottle in front of him. "All right. Where did we leave off?"

Liam is more talkative for the rest of the class, and I forget all about Jordan's remark until we're leaving.

"Have a good weekend," Liam says.

"You too. Good luck at your games." I have the hockey team's schedule memorized, so I know they're traveling Friday and Saturday for away games.

His smile dims ever so slightly. It's such a small change. I think it's only because I've watched him so long that I'm able to notice. I steal a glance at Jordan. He's watching for his friend's reaction, too. I've hit a sore spot, which obviously isn't what I wanted.

He recovers quickly, and his mouth pulls into a forced smile. "Thanks, Daisy. See you next week."

Jordan tips his head to me and departs with him.

"Stupid, stupid," I mutter softly as I head in the opposite direction.

I meet up with the girls at the cafeteria for dinner. Violet is in full-on planning mode for the ball. She flips through images from her Pinterest board, showing us everything from table designs to a photo background. As I suspected, she's gone way overboard.

Jane is all about it, and Dahlia is busy cramming in homework. She has the craziest schedule of the four of us since she is on the golf team. They have practices in the afternoons and workouts in the evenings or mornings, sometimes both.

So, while my friends are preoccupied, I think about Liam. I can't believe I was so stupid to bring up hockey when Jordan had just told me that was why he was upset. I guess I didn't really believe that was all it could be. I know student-athletes take their sports seriously, but even on bad days, Dahlia seems more like herself than Liam did during lab.

"Everything is still good with the flowers?" Violet asks me, shaking me from my thoughts.

"Yes." I take a drink of water. I've said so few words during this dinner my throat is dry. "She can deliver everything that Saturday afternoon, or we can pick it up as soon as Friday on the weekend of the event."

"Saturday afternoon?" Violet's eyes widen. "That's too late."

I nod. Hence the need for a backup plan—aka picking it up ourselves.

"I don't think you understand how many flowers we're talking about here, Daisy," she says.

"So, we'll take more than one trip."

I look to Jane and Dahlia for backup.

"I don't think we have a vehicle big enough for the archway," Jane says. "Unless it comes apart somehow."

"It doesn't," Violet says. "We need a van or a truck or something."

I hadn't thought of that. Honestly, I've given the flowers very little thought at all beyond the specific instructions Violet gave me. But I can practically see the stress rising as her shoulders lift toward her ears.

"I will figure it out," I say. When she doesn't look convinced, I add, "I will. Leave it to me."

"Thank you." She exhales.

"Why are you putting so much pressure on this? We had a blast last year, and it wasn't nearly this…" I search for a word that doesn't make her extreme planning seem negative.

"Decadent?" Dahlia offers, looking up from her homework.

"Yes, that." I point to her.

"Because…" The energy around Violet shifts as she struggles to put her feelings into words. She gets this way when she's really passionate about something. "For one night, I want our friends to feel like they are part of something as amazing and unique as they are. How many times have we been turned away or left out because we're not cool enough or outgoing enough or don't have the right friends? It's dumb. We're awesome. I want this party to be so incredible that people are begging to be invited."

"That's sweet, Vi." Also, slightly delusional. "The flowers will be there Saturday morning."

She tilts her head to the side and narrows her gaze.

"I mean Friday night." I smother a laugh.

"Thank you." She smiles. "Dahlia, do you have the fliers?"

"Yeah. They're in my backpack." She stops working to pull out a stack of fliers.

"They turned out amazing," Vi squeals and hands Jane and me each one to examine.

I groan when I see the bold title. "Wallflower Ball? You're officially calling it the Wallflower Ball?"

"Wallflowers are awesome," Jane says.

The fliers are amazing. Dahlia designed them with girls in big gowns and fierce pantsuits—a mix of her and Violet's designs. And around them a big, floral archway like the one causing the current floral nightmare.

Violet divides the stack into four. "We should post these around campus, and I have the digital file we can post online."

"Where?" I ask.

"We split up. I'll take the dorms. Daisy, take the library and University Hall. Jane can get the theater and music buildings, and Dahlia can get the rec center and athletic facilities. Anything else, we'll hit together tomorrow afternoon."

"Can I take the dorms? Or at least Freddy?" I ask as I wrap my fingers around the fliers.

"Sure," Violet says the word slowly. "Why? What are you up to?"

"Nothing. I need to talk to someone from class that lives in the building, so I'll be there anyway."

My friends are quiet for too long, and my face gets hot.

"Doesn't *Liam* live in Freddy dorm?" Violet's smile widens, and she bats her lashes.

Dahlia and Jane are watching me expectantly for more information.

With a smile, I stand. "See you guys back at the house."

Sitting and talking about him will talk me out of my plan. And the plan isn't half bad.

Freddy dorm is where most of the jocks live. Even a lot of the upper-class students stay here instead of moving out. The dorm is one of the nicest on campus, and the setup is in suites with two or four bedrooms and shared living space.

I only know this because it was in the housing packet when I was accepted to Valley U. I didn't know then it was reserved for student-athletes, but I should have guessed as much.

In high school, well-meaning guidance counselors and teachers tell you that in college, it's less about labels like jock and nerd and more about finding your people. They were half right. It was easy to find my people here. By the second semester, I had a group of people I called friends. They are all physics or art majors or girls from the same dorm hall. Then Violet, of course, once she stopped hanging with her sorority roommate. The point is the division in groups still exists. I guess because there are more of us, we're supposed to stop caring.

I haven't, but as I walk through the front entrance of Freddy, I wish I could. If just for a few minutes, I would love to be blissfully unaware that I am different than the other people walking in.

A girl in a Valley U volleyball tank top holds the door open for me and smiles. "Coming in?"

"Thanks." My gaze sweeps over the large lounge area.

Girls and guys hang out in front of a TV. The sound is muted on a basketball game, and there's music coming from somewhere—upbeat, party music. Which is exactly what it feels like—a fun, little Thursday afternoon party. Our dorm lounge never felt like that.

"Are you looking for someone?" she asks as I pause, still looking for which direction to go.

"Is there a bulletin board for announcements?"

She points to the left side near mailboxes and the front desk.

"Thanks again."

With a nod and a smile, she bounces away from me, ponytail swaying with each step.

I hang the flier and then hesitate on my plan. I don't know what floor Liam is on or if I can even get there without being stopped. Freddy is a co-ed dorm, but I don't know which are boys' floors and which are girls'. This was a terrible idea.

Not to mention, how am I going to ask him to haul something for me, therefore admitting I know he drives a truck when I have no reason to have that knowledge. No reason except when he's around, I have some sort of sense. I can spot him across campus, across parking lots... I just see him. But, yeah, I don't think that explanation is going to convince him to help me. More like run far, far away.

I'm about to leave when Jordan walks through the front doors. I look behind him, hopefully for Liam. I'm not that lucky.

His black backpack hangs on one shoulder, and his Valley Hockey hat is turned backward. He has this ease about him, from the way he dresses to the way he walks like he doesn't give a single fuck about anything. I admire it as much as I dislike it. Would it kill him to care a little about something?

It should say something about my feelings for Liam that I'm able to put one foot in front of the other and catch Jordan before he reaches the stairs.

"Jordan," I call his name, then quicken my steps to a jog so he can hear me over the music. "Jordan, hey!"

He glances over his shoulder while still moving up the stairs, but when he sees me, he stops, and his brows lift. "Daisy?"

The confusion on his face isn't malicious, but I still pray for the floor to swallow me up. I'm the last person he expected to see here.

"Hey," he says when I don't respond. "What are you doing here?"

"I..." My explanation is stuck somewhere inside of me. Why did I think this was a good plan?

"If you're looking for Liam, he isn't back yet. He had a meeting with Coach."

"Thanks." I spin on my heel to flee, but I can't seem to force myself to go. I came here for a reason, and I need to see it through or die of embarrassment trying. Spinning back around, I face him again. "Do you know what time he'll be back?"

"No, but it shouldn't be too long. You can wait for him if you want or if it's something with physics, I can probably figure it out."

"It isn't about physics."

"I figured." He flashes the smallest of grins. He tips his head, motioning for me to follow, and bounces up each stair, somehow moving slowly but energetic at the same time.

I keep a two-step difference between us as he leads me up to the fifth floor. He holds open the door for me, forcing me to go ahead of him. I stop and let him retake the lead. Lots of doors are open, letting the noise from the rooms bleed out into the hallway—music, video games, laughter. Two guys are tossing a football the length of the hall.

"Heads up," Jordan says as we pass them. "Hey, Ry."

"Thatcher." The guy he called Ry smiles and holds the football in one giant palm. "How's it going?"

"Good, man."

Ry gives me a knowing smirk that takes me a second to decipher, but when I do, I once again wish I could disappear. Ry thinks I'm on my way to hook up with Jordan. *Kill me now.*

Jordan eventually stops about halfway down the long hallway and opens a door on the left side. He walks in, holds the door open with an elbow, and flips on the light.

I'm staring at a living area. A couch and a chair face a TV with various gaming systems. Hockey jerseys hang on the wall, there are skates, sticks, and other gear shoved next to the TV, and it smells a little like a gym locker, but it's not as messy as I might have imagined.

On either side of the living area are what I assume are the bedrooms, but I can't see inside of either.

"It's even bigger than I expected," I say.

Jordan's lips pull into a wide smile.

"The room," I grit out.

"I knew what you meant."

"Then why are you smirking like that?"

"Knew what you meant, but I still thought it was funny." He drops his backpack onto a chair and points to another empty seat. "You can sit if you want."

I do and then instantly regret it. Jordan rubs the back of his neck like he's not sure how to entertain me now that I'm here. The movement lifts the hem of his T-shirt to expose an inch of flat stomach above his jeans. He's about the same height as Liam, but Jordan is leaner, and his muscles are more defined.

He disappears into the bedroom on the left side. "Do you want something to drink? We have Powerade or beer."

He comes back with one of each.

"No thanks."

He sets the Powerade on the coffee table anyway and opens the beer. He moves his backpack out of the other chair and takes a seat.

"What's that?" he asks, nodding to the fliers in my hand.

I shove the forgotten fliers into my bag. "Nothing. What time did you say Liam would be back?"

"I'm not sure." He shrugs. "I could pass on a message if you want."

"I'd really rather just ask him myself."

"Okay." He leans back and extends one long leg. "Physics and art, huh? How does that happen?"

"My parents are physicists, and art makes me feel beautiful."

Jordan stays quiet as he studies me. My answer feels too heavy. It's definitely more than he bargained for. It's the truth, but not something I usually tell people.

I fidget with my hands in my lap. "What about you? Why did you choose civil engineering?"

"Do you really want to talk about our majors?"

"*You* brought it up."

He's quiet a beat and then says, "I like being outside, and engineers make decent money. It's a good fallback plan."

"Fall back from what?"

He takes a drink of his beer. "I was drafted by the Kings over the summer."

I don't immediately put it together until he adds, "They're a pro hockey team."

"Oh. Wow. Congrats."

"Thanks."

Silence falls between us again. He taps his finger on the side of his beer can. "Are you sure I can't pass on the message? I could write it down and everything."

Standing, I start to move past him. "I should get out of your hair. I'll just send him an email or something."

He grabs my hand to stop me. The pads of his fingers are warm and calloused, and an unexpected thrill shoots up my arm. He smells like soap and beer.

I pull away first.

Jordan brings his hands together, gliding his palms together slowly in front of him. "Don't go. Stay, have a drink. I'll text Liam and see if he's on his way yet."

6

JORDAN

"He's leaving the rink now."

Daisy's blonde head bobs, eyes downcast. "Thank you."

Her fingers wrap around the red bottle. She hasn't taken a drink, but she looks maybe the slightest bit more at ease. What the hell am I doing, letting her get comfortable and practically rolling out the red carpet for her to ask out Liam?

The last thing he needs is another distraction. The past week he's gone from bad to worse. And if it were only impacting him, that'd be one thing, but the whole team is suffering.

Besides, the more time I spend with him and Daisy in class, the less I can see them together. I mean, the guy spent the entire two hours of class moping while sitting next to a girl who just wanted him to pay attention to her. He's too caught up in his own shit to see how much she likes him.

"What did you mean today?" Daisy asks with the slightest edge to her voice.

When I look at her, she's no longer staring at her feet but right at me. She has these big blue eyes and dark lashes that are hard to look away from when she has them trained on me.

"When you said that you wouldn't expect me to understand about Liam and hockey," she clarifies.

"Oh, uh, nothing. He had a rough day. Practice was awful, and Coach was on his case. I wouldn't take anything he did or said today personally."

"The only thing I took personally was you implying I couldn't possibly understand. Is that some sort of dig at my intelligence?"

A chuckle escapes, but the look she cuts me has me reining it back. "No, of course not."

"I'm a straight-A student."

"I'm not surprised."

"So?"

She's pretty cute all wound up. In class, she seems all timid, but I like the fire in her eyes now.

"Have you ever been on a sports team?"

"No." Her shoulders stiffen.

"Then you don't know what it's like to be a part of something, have people depend on you, and then fail them."

"Liam feels like he's failing the team. Why?"

"Do you follow the games at all? Never mind, it doesn't matter. Liam is in a funk. As our captain, he needs to lead us even when he's not playing well. He's still figuring it out."

"You're right. I don't get it. I mean, I understand, but that doesn't sound fair. Because he's not playing well, the team blames him for the losses? Isn't the whole point of a team that you're stronger together? If he were playing well, you wouldn't say he won you the game. Why should a loss be blamed on a single guy?"

I mull that over. It isn't exactly the way I'd put it, but she isn't wrong either. No one is blaming Liam for us losing. We just know we can be a hell of a lot better with him playing well.

Before I can respond, the door opens, and Liam walks in.

"Hey." His gaze goes straight for Daisy and his face breaks out into a wide smile. "What are you doing here?"

She stands and pink dots her cheekbones. "Hi."

An awkward beat passes before she blurts out, "I'm sorry to drop in like this. I have sort of a favor to ask."

"Sounds interesting." Liam continues to smile at her. "Let me just toss my stuff in my room."

I guess that's my cue. Liam comes back out and sits next to her on the couch. That's the last thing I see before I stand and start toward my room to give them some privacy.

Sitting at my desk, I open my laptop to do homework. Liam's voice carries through the thin wall, but I can't make out Daisy's quieter words. Adrenaline vibrates under my skin. What are they talking about out there?

"Yeah," Liam says so enthusiastically that a pit forms in my stomach.

She did it. I can't believe she did it. She actually asked him out. Damn, I knew I shouldn't have invited her up. *Fuck.*

Daisy's voice climbs as she thanks him. I stare at the screen of my laptop, then snap the lid closed. Their voices move closer, and the door to the hallway opens. Leaning back in my chair, I can see Liam standing with the door held open and the slightest sliver of her dark blonde hair in front of him. I push back a little more until I can see her through the crack in the door. She has a nice smile. Full lips hide straight, white teeth. When the corners of her mouth pull high enough, she gets a cute little smile wrinkle on the left side of her cheek.

Balancing on the back two legs of the chair, I tilt back another inch to watch as Liam steps closer. It'd be a bold and uncharacteristic move for him to kiss her, but my heart stops as I wait to see how far he'll go. His arms lift at the same time my legs go over my head, and I'm unceremoniously dropped on my head.

I curse the chair and groan as I pick myself up. She's gone by the time I glance toward the door again.

"Everything okay in here?" Liam steps into my room and eyes the chair overturned in front of my desk.

"Fine." I right the chair and rub my elbow. "Daisy left already?"

"Please." He sits on the end of my bed. "Like you weren't in here eavesdropping."

Sitting back at my desk chair, I smile. "She talks too damn quiet. I assume you said yes?"

A deep laugh leaves my buddy. "Yeah, it's no problem. It'll only take an hour or two."

His shrug is so blasé I struggle to find the words. "Only take an hour or two? I'm confused. That's a good thing?"

He tilts his head to the side. "What is it you think she asked me to do for her?"

"To go out on a date. What else?"

His shoulders and chest shake with laughter before I hear it.

I toss a pencil at him. "What the hell is so funny? She's obviously into you."

"You think?"

"It's painful to watch someone be so oblivious," I tell him. "Yes, that little mouse just tracked you down and waited for you to get home so she could... well, fuck, I don't even know what now. But whatever she asked, what she was really hoping for, was a date."

"That sounds better than what I signed us up for." One side of his mouth lifts. "She needs a couple of strong guys to move some flowers for an event in January."

"Oh." I can't hide my surprise. "That's it?"

Liam nods. "Yeah, man. That's it."

I take in a deep breath and lean back in my chair. "You're not going out with her then?"

He shakes his head and gets to his feet. He gives my door two taps on his way out, then takes a step back inside my room. "By the way, she said to tell you the answer is Pascal's Law."

"The answer to what?"

"I'm not sure. That's all she said. PlayStation?"

"Nah, I need to finish a couple of assignments before we leave tomorrow."

"Cool." He leaves my room for real this time, and I open my laptop and type Pascal's Law into the search engine. I know it, of course, but I don't understand what she's trying to tell me.

I pace the room, equal parts annoyed and intrigued. I really do have some homework to finish up before the bus pulls out tomorrow for Utah, but I can't focus on anything else but Daisy's cryptic message.

I pull up my email and type her name into the directory. Daisy Johnson.

From: jthatcher@valleyu.edu
To: djohnson3@valleyu.edu
Subject: Pascal
I give up. How is Pascal's Law the answer? And what was the question anyway?

I grab another beer and wait for her reply, hitting the refresh every thirty seconds.

From: djohnson3@valleyu.edu
To: jthatcher@valleyu.edu
Subject: Re: Pascal
The question is how to stop putting the pressure of success on one man's shoulders. Hence, Pascal.

Hence? Seriously.

From: jthatcher@valleyu.edu
To: djohnson3@valleyu.edu
Subject: Re: Re: Pascal
I don't think Pascal's Law works in this situation, but I'd love to hear your take.

I pull up the assignment for my strength of materials course and read it over, but as soon as an email notification pops up, I click over to read her response.

From: djohnson3@valleyu.edu
To: jthatcher@valleyu.edu

Subject: Re: Re: Re: Pascal
I was simply trying to say that maybe if you all took a little of the pressure, instead of piling it on one guy's shoulders, the team would be the better for it. Pressure applied to any part of the boundary of a confined fluid is transmitted equally in ALL directions. You all have to take some of the stress.
I know, I know. Don't @ me. A hockey team isn't a fluid, but it's the best I could do on the fly.
Go, team go!

I laugh, picturing her face typing out that cheery last line. I doubt she's ever gone to a single sporting event. But, at this point, I might even take an unathletic physics major's advice if it'll help Liam.

7

DAISY

Violet comes into my room Friday afternoon as I'm sketching. "We're going out in thirty minutes."

"Where?" I drop my pencil and smooth my hair back out of my face. I blink several times to focus my eyes after staring at the paper for so long.

Instead of answering, she comes around to look at my drawing. "What are you working on?"

I flip the paper. "You can't see yet. Not until it's done."

"You always say that." She rolls her eyes playfully.

"Then you should know better than to ask."

Smiling, she motions toward my left cheek. "You have black all over your face." Her gaze drops to the side of my right hand, and the black smudges. "Shower and meet us downstairs for a drink before the Uber gets here."

"You didn't say where we were going?" I call after her.

I see Dahlia as I'm heading to the bathroom. She yawns and stretches like she just woke up from a nap.

"Do you know where we're going?"

"No idea," she says. "How much are Violet and Jane going to yell at me if I just wear this?"

She's in a baggy white T-shirt and jeans. She looks great, but maybe a little wrinkled. Our friends treat nights out like a runway show. I guess it's because we don't do it that often that it always feels like a lot of pressure to look and dress a certain way.

"I could do your hair if you want," I offer.

"Distract them with killer hair and makeup." Dahlia grins. "I love it."

The four of us meet in the kitchen downstairs five minutes before the Uber is supposed to arrive.

Jane gives me an appreciative once over when I walk into the room. "Wow. Daisy. You look great."

She circles around me, taking in every detail. I feel so short next to her.

Jane is five foot eight without heels, but she's almost always wearing heels, so she looks even taller. She's technically a freshman, but she's the same age as the rest of us. She took a year off before starting school.

She's a music major and filthy rich. Not just rich like she had nice things growing up. Jane has the kind of money that makes her a little out of touch with reality. Her parents are... well, actually I don't know what they do, but something that makes them very wealthy. She once tried to offer me a thousand dollars to help her study for a calculus test.

She isn't snooty, and she doesn't really care about labels, though I think her shoe collection is mostly Louis Vuitton—even her sneakers.

Dahlia met her when she came to tour Valley U last spring. They kept in touch over the summer, and we jumped at the chance for all four of us to move in together off-campus this year.

"Will you please tell me where we're going now?" I ask Violet.

She grins. "The Hideout."

My stomach drops. "We can't drink at The Hideout. They've been cracking down hard on underage drinking, and I'm shit at lying."

"Don't worry. I've got us covered." She pours us each a shot of tequila. "And, despite all my strongly worded emails to the owner, I can almost guarantee that the TVs will be tuned in to watch your guy play Utah."

All three look at me.

"He isn't my guy." My face suddenly feels hot. "We're just lab partners."

I hold out my shot glass, and we clink them together, then toss them back. A shiver rolls through me at the awful liquor.

"For now," Jane says, her face still twisted up from the tequila. "But who knows, by the end of the night anything could happen."

"Exactly!" Vi exclaims. "Although he is a jock. Maybe we can find you someone else tonight."

"And you're both already drunk," I say as I take the shot glasses and put them in the sink.

The Hideout is a classic restaurant and sports bar. On the bar side, Valley students are jammed into tables and booths and every space in between, making it hard to walk through, let alone find a spot to sit down.

Jane stands taller than the rest of us and scans the bar area for somewhere to sit.

"There's a table in the back right," she says and makes a beeline for it.

A frazzled server approaches us as soon as we sit down, then gets shoved into the end of the table by a group passing by. It's vicious in here tonight.

"Can I get you something to drink?" She blows her hair out of her eyes.

"A bottle of your most expensive wine," Jane says with a dispassionate glance in the direction of our server.

"I need to see your IDs."

Jane sighs, and her posture loosens. "Just a glass of tonic for me. Lime on the side."

"Sprite," Violet says.

Dahlia orders the same, and then our server looks at me.

"Diet—"

Someone kicks me under the table.

"Ouch," I yelp.

"Sorry. My foot slipped," Violet's voice is sugary-sweet, but her eyes are wide like she's trying to communicate something.

"Diet Coke," I repeat. "Thanks."

"Got it." The server disappears, and I lean forward to rub my shin.

"Ow, Vi. That really hurt. I think I already have a bruise."

"I'm sorry, but I was trying to get you to order something that would mix a little better."

Jane lifts a bottle of alcohol from her purse on the seat between her and Violet and then hides it again.

"So the wine was just to throw her off?"

"No," Jane says, leaning forward on an elbow, so her diamond bracelet catches the light. "I really was hoping for wine, but I brought back up." Her words get quieter as the server reappears.

"Wow, that was fast," Violet says.

"You're my last table, and I am eager to get out of here," she says and sets our drinks on the table in the same order. "I'm closing out. Jordan will help you if you need anything else."

My head snaps up, and I instinctively look for him, only realizing she doesn't mean Jordan Thatcher but an entirely different Jordan that works here. He's been on my mind, though. The other Jordan. He and Liam, of course.

The game is on, but the angle to the TV is weird, and the players look like blurry dots on the small screen.

"Drink up, ladies," Jane says.

We make room in our glasses, and then she adds alcohol to each of our drinks.

I take a long sip and cough. "What is that?"

"Vodka."

"I tried to get you to pick something other than Diet Coke," Violet says. She takes a small sip from my glass and grimaces. "We need to order you something else after you drink that."

But by the time I get to the end of the glass, I've almost gotten used to the taste. And I'm definitely tipsy. It's been a while since the four of us have gone out together. Even living together, I don't see them as much as I thought I would when we moved in at the start of the year.

Dahlia is busy with golf, Violet is busting her butt this semester to put together a portfolio for an internship next summer, Jane volunteers with a local youth music program, and I'm just me.

Dahlia is the most like me, but without Violet and Jane, we'd be two sad friends staring at one another every weekend, wishing the other would force us out of our shells.

I think that's the thing people don't realize about being shy. Most shy people desperately want to be included, but to do something as simple as plan a night out makes us anxious. We tell ourselves a thousand stories of how awful it could go and decide the payoff isn't worth it.

It's different when Violet is with me. She understands me. She protects me. Which gives me the confidence to say and do things I might not otherwise. Being the shy girl doesn't mean I'm always quiet. Just when I feel out of my element or like I have a lot on the line. Like talking to Liam.

When it's time for new drinks, Dahlia and I weave through people to get to the bar. Jordan, not Thatcher, hasn't stopped by our table once. I can't really blame him since we're not ordering food or alcohol.

Two bartenders are working. It's busy, but even the people coming up after us get waited on before us. Frustration builds. I stand a little taller and plead (mentally, of course) for one of them to notice us. Dahlia and I share a sympathetic smile.

"We might be here a while," she says.

Nodding, I glance up at the TV hanging behind the bar. It's the third period, and Valley is up by one. The camera zeros in on Jordan, coming off the ice and tapping his glove with a teammate. Sweat makes his dark hair curl around his helmet. His cheeks are red, and there's an intensity in his eyes that's so different than the easy, playful one I've seen so often. I think I spot Liam's blond head, but the camera moves on before I can get a good look.

"What is taking so long?" Violet asks, coming up behind me. She lifts an arm to get the bartender's attention, which she succeeds in almost immediately.

We leave a minute later with fresh drinks.

Valley wins the game, but I only know because the bar is loud with cheers and applause at the final buzzer.

"I bet your boyfriend is happy," Violet says. Her teasing gets infinitely worse when she's drunk.

"He is not my boyfriend."

"Not yet," Dahlia bumps my elbow.

"Tell me again what he said when you went to his dorm?" Jane asks.

"I still can't believe you just showed up there," Dahlia says.

"I probably would have chickened out, but I ran into Jordan on his way up."

"Oh, right," Jane says. "I forgot they were roommates. They're so different."

They fire questions at me after I retell the story.

"What was their dorm like?"

"When are you going to see him again?"

"Are you like friends with him now?"

"Does this mean we'll be invited to the hockey parties?"

"We're not friends," I say. "Aside from the favor, I've only talked to them during class. And Jordan and I exchanged a few emails."

Their eyes pique with interest, and I wave them off. "It was silly."

When it's clear they aren't going to stop staring at me until I tell them about the emails, I do. And then they spend the next thirty minutes talking about Jordan and the many rumors they've heard about girls he's hooked up with. The list is long, but I already knew that.

"You didn't tell me about Jordan," Violet says later when the two of us make a trip to the ladies' room.

"It was nothing."

"It doesn't sound like nothing." Her gaze narrows. "Do you have a thing for him now?"

"Jordan?" My screech gets the attention of two girls entering the restroom. I lower my voice as butterflies swarm in my stomach. "No, of course not. He's... no."

But he is intriguing and not exactly who I pegged him to be. He's playful and witty and even polite. He could have sent me away or made me feel like a real idiot for sitting around waiting for Liam, and instead, he sat there and talked with me until Liam got back. I always imagined him as Liam's opposite, but I'm not sure that's entirely true.

After another drink, the four of us head back to our house to watch movies and play dress up. It's Violet and Jane's favorite thing to do after a night out. Vi brings out her latest creations, and she and Dahlia play designer, dressing Jane and me from head to toe. It's kind of awesome.

"Wine or stick with vodka?" Violet asks, pulling both from the fridge.

"Wine," Jane says at the same time Dahlia says, "Vodka."

With a laugh, Violet puts them on the counter. "Help yourself."

Jane and Dahlia fawn over Violet's newest designs, and I take my vodka and Sprite to the living room and scroll through my phone. I pull up the email exchange from Jordan and re-read it.

I hit reply and then tap my thumb on the edge of my phone, unsure what to say. I lock my phone and set it on the couch beside me. Liam gave me his number to contact him about the flowers, but I can't make myself text him randomly even to say congrats.

My pulse thrums dangerously. I take a large gulp of my drink and grab my phone.

From: djohnson3@valleyu.edu
To: jthatcher@valleyu.edu
Subject: Congrats!
I heard Valley won tonight. Congratulations.

8

JORDAN

WE'RE STAYING in Utah tonight. The bus leaves early in the morning, and we have another game tomorrow in northern Arizona before we head back to Valley late Saturday night.

Liam snores lightly from his bed on the opposite side of the room. I pull on my headphones and turn on music, but sleep isn't in the cards yet. I'm keyed up from the game. We finally pulled out a win. It wasn't pretty, but we did it.

Scrolling through my phone, I respond to texts from my mom congratulating me on the game, then check email.

"No way," I mutter under my breath. I click on the new message from Daisy. Something like excitement bubbles under the surface as I read her few words. I check the timestamp. Only ten minutes ago.

Fuck it. I'm bored and a long way from sleeping.

From: jthatcher@valleyu.edu
To: djohnson3@valleyu.edu
Subject: Re: Congrats!
Thanks. I guess all we needed was a little bit of Johnson's Law. What are you up to tonight?

I send it and wait.

From: djohnson3@valleyu.edu
To: jthatcher@valleyu.edu
Subject: Johnson's Law?
I'm hanging out with some friends. I think you meant Pascal's Law. How'd that work out?

From: jthatcher@valleyu.edu
To: djohnson3@valleyu.edu
Subject: Yes, JOHNSON'S Law
Pascal's Law was a stretch, but I took your advice and chatted with the guys about us all stepping up and helping lead. It might have been a fluke, but it worked tonight.
What are you and your friends getting up to?

I try to picture her out at a party in her cute little dresses, hiding in the corner.

From: djohnson3@valleyu.edu
To: jthatcher@valleyu.edu
Subject: Re: Yes, JOHNSON'S Law
Drinking and playing dress up. Are you on a bus or something?

Drinking? Interesting. I wouldn't have thought that's how she spends a Friday night. And not because she's shy. Tons of quieter people come to parties and stand off to the side, but I've never seen Daisy at a party. And I've been to plenty of them thrown by all sorts of groups of people.

From: jthatcher@valleyu.edu
To: djohnson3@valleyu.edu
Subject: Dress up?
I'm going to need an explanation. What does that mean, dress up? Halloween is over. Or is this like cosplay? I'm intrigued. Tell me more.

We're at the hotel in Utah. Back on the bus in the morning.

From: djohnson3@valleyu.edu
To: jthatcher@valleyu.edu
Subject: Re: Dress up?
My roommate is a fashion design major. She makes a lot of dresses and skirts inspired by the Regency and Victorian eras. I suppose that could be considered cosplay, but we just do it for fun after a night out.

From: jthatcher@valleyu.edu
To: djohnson3@valleyu.edu
Subject: Re: Re: Dress up?
What in the hell are dresses inspired from the Regency and Victorian eras? Like big ass dresses with corsets and shit?

Her next email says nothing, but she attaches a picture of herself in a red dress with sleeves that hang off her shoulders. It dips low in the front, pushing up her small tits.

I never noticed how little she is, but the fabric wraps tight around her midsection and then flares out around her hips. The skirt has a large slit that comes up high on her thigh, and attached to her feet are these strappy gold shoes that tangle around her legs. She looks... well, she looks fucking hot.

She's not smiling, but her lips are coated a shiny pink, and her dark blonde hair falls around her shoulders. She's a tiara away from looking like a sexy, vintage princess. It annoys me, but I can't stop staring.

Heat rushes to my dick. Man, away games are the worst. Short of picking up a random at the hotel, there's no one to hook up with after games. I could use a release right now.

I can't say any of the things I'm thinking, but I'm hella fascinated to know more now. This is not the Daisy I've been sitting next to for the past few weeks. Sure, she always looks cute, but this... fuuuuck.

From: jthatcher@valleyu.edu
To: djohnson3@valleyu.edu
Subject: Re: Re: Re: Dress up?
Your roommate made that? There's more?

From: djohnson3@valleyu.edu
To: jthatcher@valleyu.edu
Subject: My friends are talented
Yep. My cousin, Violet. Do you like them?

She's attached more pictures. Her friends, I presume. I scroll back up to the one of just her. *Damn*. Look, a sexy little dress alone doesn't make a chick hot. Her friends are wearing similar things, and they all look great. Totally fuckable by just about any guy I know standards.

But that dress on Daisy. It's just so… unexpected.

From: jthatcher@valleyu.edu
To: djohnson3@valleyu.edu
Subject: Re: My friends are talented
Yeah, that's pretty cool. Now that you're all dressed up, what's the plan? Hitting after hours?

From: djohnson3@valleyu.edu
To: jthatcher@valleyu.edu
Subject: Re: Re: My friends are talented
No, we're in for the night. This could go on for hours. Violet just opened another bottle of wine.
P.S. Diet Coke and Vodka do NOT mix well.

From: jthatcher@valleyu.edu
To: djohnson3@valleyu.edu
Subject: Drunk Daisy?
Are you drunk, sweet Daisy? I can't tell.

From: djohnson3@valleyu.edu
To: jthatcher@valleyu.edu
Subject: Re: Drunk Daisy?
I am not sweet, but I am drunk. I think. My insides are warm and tingly. Do you get your own rooms at the hotel, or are you bunked up with a bunch of other guys?

From: jthatcher@valleyu.edu
To: djohnson3@valleyu.edu
Subject: Re: Re: Drunk Daisy?
Warm and tingly, huh? Yeah, I'd say you're drunk, sweet Daisy.
Nah, just one roommate on away games most of the time. He's sleeping.

I know she's probably asking specifically about Liam. Actually, it's probably why she emailed me at all. The thought puts a bitter taste in my mouth, and I glance over at my buddy sleeping.

Something like guilt pricks the back of my neck. I'm not doing anything wrong. So we're exchanging a few emails? It's a far cry from anything I should feel bad about. I'm not stepping on his girl. He's had plenty of time to make a move. Though that might be because of what I said when he mentioned asking her out.

I scroll up to take one more look at her in the red dress and then turn my phone on silent for the night.

WE GET BACK to Valley Saturday night with another win in the books.

"Are you coming out?" I ask Liam as we step out of the bus. A few of the guys are going to the bar, and others are heading to one of our senior's, Brad McCallum's, apartment.

Liam's smile is a little quicker tonight. He still struggled out on the ice, but we found ways to score without him. I hope it's taken a little pressure off him, and he can get back to playing awesome hockey. I know what it means to him. He wants to play professionally but hasn't been drafted yet.

"Yeah, I think I'll head to the bar for a beer or two. You?"

"I told McCallum I'd stop by."

"All right, man." He offers his hand, and I take it and pull him in for a one-arm hug. "See you later. Nice job this weekend, Cap."

McCallum's apartment is already packed when I arrive. Dallas, a sophomore goalie, tosses me a beer, and I take a seat next to him at the dining room table currently covered in cards and cans.

A hand snakes down my shoulder and onto my chest. Cybil leans forward, and her shiny, brown hair falls into my face. "Hey, handsome."

"Hey." I lean back and wrap an arm around her waist, and she moves to sit on my lap.

"You missed the most epic of parties last night. I hate hockey season." She sticks out her bottom lip.

Cybil and I have an easy friendship that often leads to sex. She's a civil engineering major, too, and parties more than anyone else I know. She's a cool chick—wild and always up for a good time.

"Then I guess we better make up for it tonight." I knock Dallas on the shoulder and motion for him to move down, so Cybil has a chair.

For the next two hours, I play catch up, drinking my weight in beer. I'm always a lightweight after a game.

"Be right back," I say after we finish a hand of poker. I get up from the table, saying hey to a few people on the way to the bathroom. I've barely got my pants unzipped when Cybil slips inside and shuts the door.

She giggles. "Oh, you really had to pee."

"Yeah, at least turn around. Spare a guy a little dignity."

She does but keeps giggling. "I heard a lot of people turned up at Sigma tonight."

"The only place I'm going after this is my bed. Maybe McCallum's bed." I am beat.

"Come with me," she whines. "A quick stop at Sigma, and then you can crash at my place."

I move to the sink to wash my hands.

"Do you like my dress? It's new." She pushes in front of me, so she's wedged between me and the vanity. It's red and has a zipper down the front. She pulls said zipper down slowly until it's past her bra.

It's a sexy dress, and Cybil has a banging body. Hooking up with her is always great, but a flash of a different red dress on a different girl stops me.

"Uhhh... another night. I think I'm done for."

"Stupid hockey season," she says, and shakes her head. "Text me if you change your mind."

She leaves me alone in the bathroom. I lock the door and then pull up the last email from Daisy. She's fucking hot, and I can't stop being aware of it.

She didn't email again to congratulate me on the victory tonight, and I don't know why I keep expecting one to show up. I start to email her but stop myself. We're not friends. She's my lab partner, and she's into Liam.

I wrap my fingers around my phone and bring it up to my forehead with a groan.

What the fuck am I doing?

9

DAISY

My laptop is open in front of me, and I navigate from the English assignment I should be working on to my email. Jordan Thatcher's name taunts me, but I don't dare click on it again.

We haven't talked since Friday night, but the humiliation is just as fresh two days later.

A dull ache presses behind my eyes, and I lean forward, head in hands.

"You looked at your email again, didn't you?" Violet asks from across the table.

"Ugh." I sit tall and take a long gulp of my energy drink. It isn't helping. Neither is the soft laughter from Violet that follows.

"There should be a law against using your phone when drinking."

"It was not that bad." She smirks. "You sent a couple of sexy photos."

A new flush creeps up my neck and my stomach rolls. Stupid technology. I groan and squeeze my eyes closed.

"*Tame*, sexy photos. It isn't like you were naked," she says.

I know she's trying to help, but every word jabs into my confidence, deflating it a little more.

"Can we just study in silence?"

"Sure. Yeah." She presses her lips together and sits back in the chair across from me. The grin on her face has been the same every time we've talked about... *shudder*. I can't even say it.

"I have to say one more thing." Violet clasps her hands together on the table. We're at the library studying, or I'm attempting to with little help from Violet. "You were having fun Friday night. More fun than I've seen you have in, maybe ever. Chalk it up to that. He's probably already forgotten about the photos. I mean, we're talking about Jordan Thatcher. He has no shortage of girls at his beck and call. Honestly, that's probably the least sexy photo he got from a girl all weekend."

That should make me feel better, but it doesn't.

"I just can't believe I have to face him in class."

I look at my cousin for another dose of encouragement. Instead, her gaze is stuck behind me, eyes wide. "You might have to face him a little sooner than that."

"What?"

I swivel around and spot him as he reaches the top of the stairs. He's alone, backpack over one shoulder, hat backward, Powerade in hand. He scans the second floor until he spots whoever he's looking for and juts his chin.

I follow his trek to a table with three other guys, including Liam.

"Did you know Liam was here?" she asks.

"No." My Liam senses are all out of whack. Stupid emails. Oh my god, did Liam see the pictures? I don't know why it didn't occur to me until now, but of course, Jordan would show him. I bet they had a good laugh. Oh man, I'm going to have to drop out of physics. Maybe out of Valley U completely.

"We should go." I close my laptop and shove it into my bag.

"No. Running away is admitting you're embarrassed."

"I *am*."

She doesn't budge. "Plus, there's a better chance of them seeing you if you get up and walk around."

That keeps me planted in my seat. I take one last covert glance at their table. Liam sits forward, smiling and nodding. Jordan leans back with a pencil behind one ear, staring at his phone. His phone. Double groan.

I have never concentrated harder on being invisible. I hunch over my laptop and focus on American literature. Every noise, every shadow behind me, sets me on edge, but I don't turn back around.

"Okay, they're leaving," Violet says sometime later.

I slink down farther in the chair.

"And they're walking, walking, almost to the stairs," Violet provides the play-by-play. "Oh, they're stopping to talk to someone."

"Guy or girl."

"Girl. Pretty. Really pretty."

Of course, she is.

"Okay. I think she's moving along. They're walking again."

My heart is racing, and I want to look so bad.

"Oh." Violet's voice squeaks, and she looks down at the table. "I think you've been spotted."

"What?!"

"Oh my god. Uhh... act natural."

"Violet." My blood turns to ice. "Please tell me they're not coming over here."

She keeps her lips closed as she mumbles, "Sorry. Can't."

"Daisy?" Liam's voice comes from behind me.

I turn slowly, shooting Violet a panicked look before I do.

"Hi!" I fake surprise as I look from Liam to Jordan, then back at Liam. "What are you guys doing here?"

"Studying," Liam responds for the both of them.

"Right." *Duh.*

"We have a killer Geotech test this week." His gaze moves past me to Violet.

I wave in her direction. "This is my cousin, Violet."

Liam takes two steps forward and extends a hand. "Liam. Nice to meet you."

"Likewise."

Her ability to play it cool is impressive. Then again, a year ago, she was partying with guys like Liam and Jordan.

"Liam and Jordan are my lab partners in physics."

Jordan smiles and tips his head in greeting. "You must be the design major."

"Yeah. That's right."

Oh, the mortification. My ears burn, and I'm certain my face is bright red.

"I saw some of your stuff. It's good." Jordan wears a smile that's neither mocking nor fake.

"Fashion design, huh?" Liam asks. "What kind of stuff do you design?"

Jordan holds my gaze until I can't take it anymore. He didn't tell Liam. I'm both relieved and surprised.

"All kinds of stuff," Violet says. "But dresses are my favorite."

Liam's phone lights up in his hand.

"That's my mom," he says, backing away. He looks at Jordan. "I'll catch you back at the dorm."

Jordan nods, and Liam waves at Violet and me. "Good to see you both."

"Bye," Violet and I say at the same time.

He hurries off, putting the phone to his ear as he reaches the stairs.

Jordan lingers, and when I turn my gaze back to him, he's watching me.

"Looks like he's in a better mood," I say.

"The wins were good for him."

"Yeah, it seems like it."

Violet leans forward and points to an empty chair.

Shaking my head, I can't get the words, *I'm sure he has places to be*, out of my mouth before he's pulling out the chair and dropping his big, intimidating frame into it.

"Which was your favorite?" she asks.

"Uh…" He looks between us.

"She means the dresses," I explain.

"Oh." He grins. "They were all pretty awesome."

Violet would never give up that easily. She keeps staring at him expectantly.

"The red one was my favorite." He glances at me as he says it.

My stomach does a thousand somersaults. Rationally I tell myself it's probably the only one he remembers, or he's just guessing, but there's something about the way he's looking at me that makes my heart race.

"That is some of my best work." Violet leans back, satisfied with his answer.

"How was the rest of your weekend?" he asks me.

"Fine. Yours?"

"Good. We got in last night and went out for a bit. Any more drinking and dressing up?" He smiles at me. Jordan Thatcher is freaking smiling at me.

I shake my head. I'm a mess, heart racing, palms sweaty, stomach still doing flips. And then there's Jordan. He always looks so comfortable, so relaxed. Then again, he wasn't the one that got drunk and sent sexy pictures.

To be fair, I wasn't trying to be sexy. Or maybe I was. The dresses are sexy, and I felt good wearing them. Some part of me wanted his approval. I can't quite wrap my brain around that. Sober, I can see how it came off, but drunk, I just wanted to be noticed. I wanted Jordan to notice me.

He sits forward. Violet's gone back to her homework, or at least she's pretending not to be listening as Jordan says, "I'm glad I ran into you."

"You are?"

"I didn't know how to say this over email, still don't." He rubs his jaw and looks more unsure than I've ever seen him. I didn't know he was even capable of that look.

"O-kay."

"Just say it," Violet pipes in, still not looking up. "Because right now, she's going through every worst-case scenario in her head."

She's absolutely right about that.

A small chuckle leaves his mouth. "Liam's a good guy."

Of all the places I thought this conversation was going, this wasn't anywhere on the list. I wait for him to continue.

"He's a little slow to pick up the vibe when someone's into him."

"I don't understand what you're saying."

He gets to his feet and shoots a grin right at me. "I'm saying, if you like him, ask him out."

Ask him out? Just like that. Is he crazy?

"But I don't—" My voice breaks off. Denying seems stupid. And even if I could get up the courage, I'd never be able to face Liam again if he said no. Lab would be unbearable, and I joke, but I can't drop it. I need that class.

Jordan takes a step away, and his smile gets softer. "He won't say no. See you Tuesday."

I SPEND the next two days thinking about the weird interaction with Jordan, and playing scenarios in my head where I do what he suggested. Even in my daydreams, I can't say the words without blushing a hideous shade of red.

I hate that my crush on Liam was so easy for him to see. Okay, fine, he'd have to be an idiot not to notice. And Jordan isn't an idiot. I haven't totally figured him out, but an idiot he is not.

Tuesday afternoon during our lunch break, Violet corners me in the kitchen as I'm packing up for my final classes of the day.

"Have you decided what you're going to do?"

"I'm not asking him out." I've told her as much the other ten times she's asked.

"You heard Jordan; he won't say no!"

My heart is galloping in my chest. "Oh, well, Jordan said it, so it must be true."

"I don't think he would steer you wrong. Which is odd because I never thought Jordan Thatcher would be the type of guy to come over and tell you to ask out a guy." She shrugs. "There was something about the way he said it. He likes you."

"Liam?"

"No, Jordan."

"Oh yeah, that's why he told me to ask out someone else. Why are you pushing me to go out with Liam anyway? You hate jocks."

Violet fidgets. She doesn't really hate Liam or Jordan or anyone that I know of, except maybe our neighbor Gavin (they have history), but she'd never approve of me dating a popular jock. When it was theoretical, she played along but now...

"It's what you want, and at least Liam is a decent one."

I grab my backpack off the chair and start for the door. "I will see you later."

"He won't say no," she yells after me.

I'm usually the first person to physics lab, but today I walk so slowly that at three minutes until class starts, I realize at this rate I'm going to be late and have to book it the rest of the way across campus. Professor Green is beginning his lecture when I open the classroom door. All eyes are on me as I slip inside.

"Sorry," I tell him as I go to my table.

Liam pulls out the extra stool next to him.

"Thanks," I whisper.

For the twenty-five minutes that Professor Green covers today's lab, all I can do is focus on breathing. Frantic energy flows through my veins, and as the seconds tick by, I recognize it as adrenaline. The dangerous kind that makes you do things that shouldn't be physically possible, like lift a car or ask out your crush.

"You may get started," Professor Green says.

Liam angles his body toward me and smiles, then starts setting up the lab. I look at Jordan for reassurance. He meets my gaze with an intensity that makes my chest tighten. Oh god. He better be right.

10

JORDAN

I CAN PRACTICALLY SEE Daisy's thoughts over her head like a thought bubble. She and Liam are working through the lab while I lead us through the instructions, per the usual.

She hasn't stopped blushing since she walked in late. Today she's wearing jeans and this oversized sweatshirt that hangs off one shoulder. It's even sexier to see her like this, knowing what she looks like all dressed up.

Tapping my pencil on the paper, I redirect my gaze to the table. She's never going to ask if I keep staring at her. And I need her to ask. Then the two of them can go out, just like they both want, and I can stop thinking about her.

The number of times I looked at her in that red dress is too many to count.

"Jordan?"

My head pops up at my name, and Liam's eyes narrow in confusion. "Everything okay?"

"Yep. Great."

"Can you read the next step then?"

I clear my throat and adjust the hat on my head. "Right."

For the rest of the class, I focus only on the handout in front of me. Well, that and Daisy's soft voice as she and Liam talk through their work. I'm no help at all. I have visions of drunk Daisy in that sexy, red dress and an irrational burn in my chest to stop her from asking out Liam and ask her out myself.

"I think that's it," Daisy says.

"We're a good team." Liam holds up his hand, and she presses her much smaller palm against it lightly.

I pack up quickly and wait for Liam. He's still chatting with Daisy, taking his sweet time. We don't have class together after this, so I don't need to wait for him, but I want to see if Daisy works up the courage to ask him out. He's obviously not going to. Which is why I told her she should ask him.

I wasn't lying. He won't say no. I don't know if he's hesitated because of what I said, or maybe he's just taking his damn time, but I decided to give them a little push.

I'm seriously regretting that now as she fiddles with the straps of her backpack. This is fucking painful.

"What time are you done with classes and everything today?" she asks him. It's her in. I can see the breadcrumbs she's laying out and smile to myself.

"This is my last class."

"Where are you headed next?"

"Probably just head back to the dorm. You?"

"I'm done for the day, too."

The three of us walk out of class, her and Liam leading the way.

She glances over at him, still clutching onto the straps of her backpack like a lifeline. "I was thinking about going to University Hall and getting coffee or something."

"Cool." He bobs his head. "I love the hot mocha."

Jesus, man, take a hint.

We continue another few steps before she summons the courage. I can see it, and I hold my breath.

Her shoulders lift and, even in profile, I can see how nervous she is. "Would you want—"

One big step puts me directly between them. "Hey, Daisy, can I talk to you for a minute?"

I take her by the elbow, and a rush of pure pleasure shoots up from my fingertips.

"Y-yeah." Her voice quivers, but I swear I see relief wash over her.

"I'll see you back at the dorm," I tell Liam, effectively dismissing him.

"Sounds good." He gives me a salute. "Later, Daisy."

"Bye," she calls after him.

I step back to give her room. The two of us stand in place. My heart is hammering like a drum in my chest.

"Is everything okay?" she asks. "You look nervous or something."

"Yeah, everything's fine. I just have a favor."

Her blue eyes bore into mine like she can see into my soul. I'm waiting for her to call me on my bullshit, but instead she asks, "A favor?"

"Mhmm." I shove my hands in my front pockets.

She buys it. Of course she does. In what world would I interrupt her and say I need a favor when I don't? Fuck my life.

"Are you going to ask me, or am I supposed to guess?"

Right. Uhh. Well, crap. I scroll through options quickly and blurt out the first thing that doesn't sound totally ludicrous. "I need you to tutor me."

She hesitates. Her pink lips part and then press into a thin line. "Favors are usually posed as questions."

"Right. Can you tutor me?"

"In physics?"

"And statistics." My throat is dry, and I clear it.

"I didn't realize you were struggling."

I don't say anything. Outright lying feels shitty, though so is asking someone to tutor you when you don't need it.

"I've never tutored anyone before. I'm not sure that I'd be any good at it."

I should give her the out. I've successfully stopped her from asking out Liam. At least for now. Was that the plan? Fuck, I don't know what I'm doing.

"How's tomorrow night?"

She thinks for a second. "Fine, I think. I'm done with classes at two. I could meet you at the library right after."

The fact that she's so accommodating just makes me feel worse for not really needing a tutor.

"Great." I start to walk off, then stop. "Oh, fuck. I have film review tomorrow night." I should have asked her to borrow a damn pen or something. "How about you give me your number, and I'll text you when I'm done?"

She looks like she might be seriously regretting agreeing to this, but she rattles off her number, and I put it in my phone under Sweet Daisy. "Perfect. I'll text you when I'm done, and I can come to you if it's easier."

She nods.

And I walk away before I say or do any more dumb shit.

THANKS FOR READING this sample of Tutoring the Player. I hope you enjoyed your time at Valley U!

xo,

Rebecca

ALSO BY REBECCA JENSHAK

Campus Nights Series

Secret Puck

Bad Crush

Broken Hearts

Wild Love

Smart Jocks Series

The Assist

The Fadeaway

The Tip-Off

The Fake

The Pass

Wildcat Hockey Series

Wildcat

Wild about You

Standalone Novels

Sweet Spot

Electric Blue Love

ABOUT THE AUTHOR

Rebecca Jenshak is a *USA Today* bestselling author of new adult and sports romance. She lives in Arizona with her family. When she isn't writing, you can find her attending local sporting events, hanging out with family and friends, or with her nose buried in a book.

Sign up for her newsletter for book sales and release news.

www.rebeccajenshak.com